The Perfect Tree

Printed in the United States of America

ISBN: 0-6157-1755-1
ISBN-13: 9780615717555

Kenneth S. Harris

The Perfect Tree

Perkins May – 2012

Dedication

For Sissy, Joe and Mom

Prologue

The Perfect Tree – A Short Story

By Alfi Mae Piper

That morning, that cold and misty morning, like most in mid-October, seemed strangely different from the rest. When the hands of the clock rolled right on past 6:30 indifferently and Mr. Bradley had yet to pass by our house, as he did so daily, I knew why the continuity of existence seemed off-balance. I was twelve at the time, and had never known a day to pass that Mr. Bradley hadn't strolled past our little home within two minutes, give or take, of 6:30 in the morning.

I was out on the front porch as usual at 6:25, wearing my school dress, my hair tied up in a ribbon, to give him the same greeting I gave him nearly every morning; my pad of scribbling – a child's attempt at poetry – in one hand, my dulling pencil in the other, and my gaze fixed anxiously on what the fog would permit me to see of the tiny dirt path that some people called a road, which led further up towards the head of Caine's Creek where Mr. Bradley lived.

Every morning he would appear just like a ghost out of the fog, a walking stick in his hand clanking repetitiously at a slow and steady pace, a dirty old brown hat perched on his head. And every morning the fog was there too. It nestled in the valley that we called home, between the large mountains that stood on either side. But that particular morning, the fog came, right on schedule, but Mr. Bradley never did.

By the time the sun had crept over the trees that stood atop the mountains, I knew he wasn't coming. He would have to wait until the next day to hear the poem I had completed just the previous evening, of which I thought to be my best to date. He always listened to my poems in the morning, showing the utmost interest. I knew he would love this one.

Excitement drained and a mixture of melancholy and acceptance took its place.

It made the walk to school seem longer with my poem in hand, still unread by my dear friend. The next day came and I waited in the cold, standing on the exact spot I had stood on the day before, knowing deep down he was not coming, but hoping as only a child can.

Sunday, at church, I sat barely hearing the words of Preacher Bryant with Mr. Bradley on my mind. Sadly enough, at that point in my life he had been my closest friend, ever since childhood. The people from school who called themselves my friends – the few that there were –

had never given any thought to anything I had ever written. They just shrugged it off as "unnecessary homework."

After lying awake for most of the night, I got up the next morning at the usual six o'clock to get ready for school, trying consciously to notice nothing outside, going nowhere near the windows and definitely nowhere near the porch. That day I set out for school, leaving my poetry notebook behind. Something I had never done.

For a reason that still baffles me, somehow I knew that Mr. Bradley had met with bad fortune. I had seen him every morning since I had started school, and he had always arrived right on schedule. It made me sick with dread.

The fog was exceptionally thick that morning as I walked at the usual safe distance behind the two Watson girls, daughters of our neighbors, feeling empty and silent inside my head. The Watson girls never said much to me. They walked to school even though their dad owned one of the few automobiles on Caine's Creek. He was likely driving the car to work, but the girls still walked with a prideful stride at knowing they were oh so close to the top of the social food chain, that they had something so many wanted but couldn't afford.

Sometimes on the way to school we would run into Mr. Bradley as he returned home from his morning walk. I loved those days when I got to see Mr. Bradley twice in one morning: before leaving for school, and along the way! The Watson sisters would lift their noses to the gray morning sky; I would stop to chat with him, falling far behind, but never showing up late. Mr. Bradley always made sure of that. But that morning, I didn't even bother to look up from the dirt and the slowly dissipating fog.

The tiny one-roomed schoolhouse came into sight and stood proudly glowing in glare of the sun. I climbed the steps to the front door and entered only a few seconds after the Watson sisters. I never showed up right behind them. Mrs. Coleman watched me with a peculiar expression as I took my seat two spaces in front of Lidia and Elizabeth Watson, next to my closest friend at school, Bruce.

Bruce was around my age, and was always nice to me, but he was also however, one of those who I could tell shrugged off my poetry – as simplistic as it may have been in those days of my youth – with recognizable ease. He was more into fishing and climbing the hills that surrounded all of our homes. Don't get me wrong, I enjoyed those things, but often longed for more. Bruce seemed to always be in a cheerful mood, and he never teased me like some of the other boys did. However, like most others that lived on Caine's Creek, he didn't think too highly of Mr. Bradley—my true best friend. Like most, he found him odd, even a little creepy. I, on the other hand, always found him to be a cheerful old man, always smiling through a thick gray beard, getting around as best as he could with the clanking of that familiar old walking stick.

"You're here early," said Bruce. "Didn't you run into that crack-pot old man this morning?"

"He's not an old crack-pot," I said calmly without looking up. "You don't even know him."

"I know what my mom and dad say about him," Bruce said, chuckling. "That he is a crazy old man who never talks to nobody. Barely even comes out of his house, 'cept to go walking in the mornings. What do you think he does up there all day, all alone in that old shack?"

I glared at Bruce. He must have known I was upset.

"I'm sorry," he said, looking abashed. "You know I was just teasing you."

"I know." And that was the truth. Bruce teased me about Mr. Bradley all the time. I knew he was teasing, but it didn't help.

I looked at him with eyes admitting sadness and shook my head before looking down at my desk.

Learning proved to be quite the difficult task that day. I have yet to forget that numb feeling that swallowed me, giving me my first taste of what it is like to lose something you truly care about. It is a lesson we all learn I suppose, but different for me because at that point in my life Mr. Bradley had been the only person, aside from my parents, that seemed to care for me, almost like the grandfather I never knew. That loss befell me with such impact that I never wanted to feel again.

He's dead, I thought. *People don't just disappear, so he has to be dead. Would anybody even know if he died alone up in that old house?*

By the end of the day, when school was letting out and I certainly felt no smarter than I had that morning, I only wanted to go home and confide to a clean sheet of paper all of the things that I had been feeling. Rain had started to sprinkle lightly upon the windows of the school about halfway through the day, and had only worsened as the day progressed, the sky growing darker, more threatening. When I stepped out the front door, I heard Mrs. Coleman – the young and meek-voiced teacher who had watched me so carefully that morning – call my name from just inside the door, where she always stood as the children departed her presence.

"Piper, you haven't seemed yourself at all today," she said. "Has something been bothering you?"

I looked up at her, feeling frightened and helpless, my spine tingling. I hesitated.

"It's just that I haven't seen or heard anything about Mr. Bradley in the past few days. I'm worried about him."

"Why are you so worried?" she asked. "I'm sure he's okay."

"Well, normally I see him every morning before school, or before Church. He reads my poems." I hesitated and swallowed hard before continuing. "But now I haven't seen him in days."

She made these eyes at me, accusing eyes that looked as though they themselves were holding a secret. Her face was disapproving at the thought of me spending time with Mr. Bradley. She feigned her usual warm smile. "I'm sure he'll turn up. Maybe he's sick, at home in bed with some bug or something."

"Maybe," I said without much hope, and walked out into the hammering rain. My stage of childish optimism for the situation had passed the previous day.

The walk home was lonely and the weather was dreadful. The dirt road had turned to mud from the persistent precipitation and the small creek at the side of it had begun to rise. These things didn't bother me. I simply shrugged them off as unstoppable change. It was such a strange feeling, walking home with such a haze over my eyes that I could barely remember how cold the rain was, or when the first drop had hit me.

I found writing to be no help either, for that feeling of emptiness that I so desperately wanted to get down was difficult, if not impossible, to put into conceivable words. I grew frustrated quickly and gave up, putting my tears on the paper instead. I sat through an almost silent supper with my parents before going to bed early, only to lay awake, eyes wide open, seeing nothing, only thinking thoughts much too dark for my age.

Sleep felt like blinking with a few hours in between, leaving my eyes heavy and sore when they opened. I walked into the living room to find the clock barely telling me through the darkness that I was up early. It was only 5:40. I dreaded another day baring this awful feeling, sitting through hours filled only with Mrs. Coleman's mannerly and informative voice, never comforting.

I returned to my room and got dressed, giving a prolonged glance to my latest poem. I was so looking forward to Mr. Bradley hearing it. Now it was just eight lines that would never be read nor heard by anyone who cared about that sort of thing. I left my room, and then the house, not leaving early for school, but for Mr. Bradley's house in the head of our little holler. My father had already left for work, and my mother had fallen to sleep again as she usually did until it was time to wake me for school, so no one noticed when I left so early.

The one-lane path was still wet and the fog had gathered just as thick as usual, and when combined with the darkness of the early hour, it made it immensely difficult to see. The trees on the sides of the path rose up out of it, looming tall and dark over me, their bare branches like tensely drawn hands, rigid and troubling. I tried not to look up. Sounds came from seemingly all around me: the sounds of nature so early, the clicking, chirping, the rustling of fallen leaves, even the occasional sound of an owl seemed like warnings. I pulled my coat tight and continued to where there were fewer houses and the path began to get smaller, where at last I would come to its end, and at the end I would find the house that belonged to Mr. Bradley. I had never been there, but everyone knew where he lived. "The old Bradley place," most people called it.

I passed the last house I would see for a while, standing dark and ghastly in the early morning air, and continued walking for at least ten minutes, past images that looked vaguely familiar: thickets of trees on both sides of the path lining the bank to the creek and then proceeding up the mountain behind it. The trees loomed over the road on both sides creating a transparent canopy of wooden fingers entwined. Then, at last, I saw it, like a shadow lengthening in approaching light, becoming less of a ghost as each of my steps brought me closer to my destination, and perhaps, hopefully, an answer. It solidified out of the darkness, from transparency to actuality. It rose up out of the fog and shadow, the last dwelling on that road. I approached it with caution, reflexively.

I was furiously hoping Mr. Bradley would be inside under a blanket, running a fever, with a cup of water and a bowl of soup at his side.

Small stone chunks, strategically placed, formed steps that led up the incline of the bank to the tiny ledge, barely big enough for the house that sat upon it. And as tiny as my feet were then, they barely fit upon those stones; caution once more.

Once at the top, the house glared down at me, its windows peering like empty eyes, black and sinister. A walkway made from stones similar to those of the steps led me to four rickety, worm-eaten wooden steps, humbled by the decay of time and use. I tried not to notice the clutter of dusty furniture on the porch: old wooden rocking chairs, a coffee table with a cup still sitting on it, and a swing on the far end hanging from the roof of the porch. These things reminded me far too much of home, but without the layer of settled dust. After a nervous glance around, I knocked on the door, praying for an answer, that Mr. Bradley was sick and that was all; nothing life-threatening or life-changing, maybe just feeling a little under the world, as I had heard him put it. I knew I shouldn't be there. But it was my only hope of ending the anticipation — meaning that it would either take the burdening weight of possibility off my mind, or ignite my worst fears and let them burn high, consuming me while constantly fueled with kindling and kerosene.

I waited, but no answer came. I knocked again, but got the same result. Holding my breath, I reached down and took the cold doorknob in my hand, turned it and it opened. At the shock of this — for I had expected it to be locked, so that I could merely turn and walk away feeling that I had tried to the fullest extent — I stood gaping in the musty smell and the air that poured out of

Mr. Bradley's home, much colder than the chill of the October dawn. I felt that the door opened by my intentions committed me to going inside, to get answers, to find my friend.

Not once however, did the thought enter my mind of finding Mr. Bradley cold and motionless on the floor, or perhaps in his bed, looking warm beneath mountains of blankets, almost peaceful, but starting to smell. No one would have come to check on him; no one would miss him, except for me of course, because he never really had anywhere to be; no one would even care enough to bury him, at least not until the stench from the house found its way further down the holler, and not without proper pay.

Such ill thoughts and intention towards my friend saddens me to this day. People can be inherently cruel; one has to try not to be, it seems.

But I didn't find Mr. Bradley, or any remnants of him. Through the heaps of tattered books and stacks of fraying pages — relentlessly scribbled — I found not one trace of my dear friend. I did, however, take the privilege of reading some of his work, wrongly so perhaps, but I could not help myself. I never even knew he had written anything, but that would explain his interest in my poems and my development as a creator of such. Actually, I had never noticed until this point that he had always seemed to know a great deal about literature, always helping me, giving me new ideas: "Perhaps you could try three stanzas instead of four," he would say. "Or maybe change your rhyme scheme here, A B B A B, and set your syllables Pip, make 'em even."

I had done so, without question, hearing an adult's literary suggestions voiced in the understanding of a child.

I know I shouldn't have, but I did. I took up a page Mr. Bradley had written that was lying on his desk. It had the stain of a coffee cup on it, a gritty dark brown ring in the upper left corner. And in the gloom of the dreary house, surrounded by the belongings of a friend I was sure I would never see again, I read:

Eyes upon me, I feel a familiar weight:
A mountain, a globe, upon my shoulders, I'm bent beneath.
If only Atlas, this world I wish not to hold.
My heartstrings pulled taut as a harpsichord
Playing a familiar song,
A song I have heard all my life,
Each note resonating brilliant sound, yet sour.

I took a few pages of Mr. Bradley's work, folded and stuffed them deep into my pocket. Rather than going to school, I spent the day in Mr. Bradley's home, reading his work, and taking in the sights of his house that I had, until that day, never seen. Finally, I made my way home in silence. On my way out the door I found a full sheet of paper tacked to the door with only a few words printed clearly upon it – "Tell Piper I'm sorry. And to keep writing."

I pocketed it and cried nearly the whole way home. I didn't know what it meant exactly, but could discern that goodbye was somewhere between the lines.

That evening, I spoke hardly a word to either of my parents. All through supper they watched me with eyes that said they knew I had not been to school that day. But they never mentioned it, and neither did I.

That evening, sitting in my tiny room perched upon my bed, eyes glazed with thought but staring intently at the wooden walls all the same, I reflected upon what I had come to call my last encounter with Mr. Bradley. It was on a Thursday morning.

He had come steadily down the road, emerging from the morning fog as usual, carrying his walking stick with the same old hat sitting on his head; nothing out of the ordinary at all. "Good mornin' Pip," he said. I returned the greeting and ran out to meet him holding two new poems firmly in hand, each page streaked with correction. "Well, let me see what ya got there," he said, taking my poems in hand and reading them with squinted eyes. Upon finishing the first he said, "Ya know, you're gonna be great one day. And I don't just mean great, but one of *the* greats. You truly have a gift Pip, especially to be so young."

"You really think so?" I said through an inescapable smile.

"Without a doubt."

I beamed at him, my smile stretching the skin on my face to a new length. To hide my reddening cheeks I hurriedly asked another simple, nothing-out-of-the-ordinary question.

"So where you off to this morning?"

"Today?" he said, his eyes drifting up to the dreary and darkening sky in which angry and oppressive storm clouds were gathering clandestinely in various shades of thick gray haze; that same haze seeming to reflect clearly in Mr. Bradley's eyes. "Today, I'm just looking for the perfect tree." And he smiled. His gaze fell on me heavily.

It is at this point that my memories of the day show me something that seemed off, out of the ordinary, unlike the other mornings chatting with Mr. Bradley. His voice seemed to carry a weight with it, like his lungs were pushing the air to make words with great difficulty, and his eyes were only open for the sake of routine. I noticed him drawing long breaths and forcing smiles — anyone can tell a forced smile from a genuine one, I believe — and I asked him what was wrong.

"I'm just feeling a little under the world today," he said.

"Like you're at the end of your rope?" I said, remembering Mama using that phrase whenever she was acting similarly to the way Mr. Bradley was acting, though not quite to the same extreme, usually over a sink of dirty dishes, a basket of dirty clothes, with her hands full with me and daddy.

"No, not quite there yet. But it feels like I might be there pretty soon," he said with a smile, a genuine smile. I returned the smile and gave Mr. Bradley his daily hug. But he held on a little tighter, a little longer that day.

I

Hemingford was a rust-red town, seeming as far from the city as one could get, trading towering buildings for towering maples. Smalltime farmers called it home, because the land was lush and well-kept, the weather consistent. It always seemed to rain when it was needed.

Tiny dirt roads that were seldom used since Hemingford was introduced to blacktop some decades back laced the landscape like tiny veins protruding from a gently beating heart. Several bicycle paths led through literal forests—an old play-haven for children, still abundantly used.

People looked down long noses at neighbors deeming everyone either a devout or a degenerate, completely oblivious to the fact that a lot of people were neither, and some both.

Blake Kiser, a 12-year-old boy who saw the world through great brown eyes that could have been 30, lived on an old farm on Crystal Creek Road, the house seated snug against a thicket of trees. There was no backyard, and the banisters of the back porch ran even with tree branches and shade.

The farm consisted of a small field of beans and corn, a couple rows of potatoes, and a barn made of bare, weathered wood. That was where they kept a few chickens, and Aphrodite, their only cow. The farm was nowhere near big enough to make a living off of, but it kept the family in a reasonable supply of eggs, vegetables and milk, though Blake's dad did make a little from time to time selling vegetables to neighbors.

To children who lived a little closer to town, the farm was old, rustic, and even a little bit creepy; to Blake it was home.

Blake lay in his bed as rain rapped persistently on the tin roof. He had considered carving or writing before bed but he was too tired. Blake had always been a reader since old enough to distinguish letters from numbers, and had taken up writing his own stories recently, though even he would admit from time to time that they weren't very good. He *was* good at carving, however—"whittling" folks around those parts called it. His dresser was lined with tiny wooden figures he had carved out of inspiration or just simple boredom.

This summer his father had dubbed him old enough to handle a little more work around the farm. A *little* more turned out to be a lot more, and for the first time in his life, Blake was glad the summer was almost over. He was used to spending summers with Matt Branham. Best friends having fun. But Matt was gone now, moved halfway across the country from Kentucky to Colorado. Blake reckoned Matt might as well be on the moon.

School started in three days. Only one weekend remained.

As he lay quietly in the darkness, Blake could still hear his mother's voice in his head, bickering about one thing or another, as she had done most of the summer: "I'm telling you kids," she would say. "I'm about at the end of my rope. You'll have to start pulling more weight around here. Life ain't supposed to be easy, you know."

It seemed that no matter how much work Blake did around the farm—hoeing rows in the garden, tilling dirt, though the rusty old tiller was nearly too rough for him, mowing the lawn, harvesting beans and stringing them up in the barn to dry—it was never enough. There was ever one more thing to get done.

He closed his eyes. His bed felt soft, yet pained his sore back. He'd barely had any fun all summer, and actually felt that returning to school would be more of a vacation than the summer break had been.

The lights were off in his room, so there was no orange glare on top of his eyelids. His room was nearly silent, but he could hear the rattle of the rain on the roof, and just barely, the indistinguishable murmuring on the TV downstairs.

Dianne, his older sister, 14-years old and proud of it, had spent the summer reading novels and plays for the fall's AP English class. She was about to bust with excitement now that school was starting back. Her chore-load had stayed the same. Their father didn't think it was a girl's place to be sweating on a farm. Blake felt betrayed, but the extra work had made him strong. In fact, he had even lost a little weight. He had always been a chubby kid; but now, when he looked down at his toes, he actually saw them instead of a perfectly round gut protruding over the waist of his jeans.

He was contemplating what another year at school would be like—being ignored by "the in-crowd," dodging spit-wads and right hooks from Ronnie Peterson and Van

Dougherty, and watching people who had a lot of friends be normal children instead of hired farmhands who made only five dollars a week because their *employer* had the audacity to call it an allowance. He pictured beautiful girls looking in any direction but his, and rides on the bus where he would change seats seven times in the 20-minute ride from his house to the school, and—

His thoughts were interrupted by a faint light outside his window. It washed over his eyelids and turned the darkness a familiar stale orange for just a moment.

The next house was a good piece away on the other side of the corn field. But in the darkness, the light on its front porch could be seen, and it seemed out of place considering no one had lived in that house for as long as Blake could remember.

He crept closer to the window. A car sat in the driveway with its headlights still on, tiny flecks of rain falling in the beams. He wondered what the people would be like, but only for a moment. Truly, he didn't really care.

***

The next day, the day some kids believe to be the last happy day until Christmas (the last Saturday before school sets back in), Blake's mother took him and Dianne into town.

With school about to start again, they both were in need of new clothes; Dianne, because she was to be a freshman at Hemingford High School and had outgrown most of her old things; Blake because he had ruined most of his clothes in the dust trail behind a tiller or in sopping around in soggy, brown earth on the farm.

The family only had one vehicle: an '84 Chevrolet pick-up that could almost pass for new, aside from the wear present in the bed and along the tailgate. The three of them slid into the front seat with ease; but should the matter arise that all four family members had to go somewhere together, it was a pretty tight squeeze.

Dianne got the seat by the window, as always. Sometimes Blake hated being the youngest, ever cast in his sister's shadow. Dianne typically got her way because of her status in school: always on the honor roll, always straight As. Blake usually got As and Bs in English, but was a steady C student in other regards. He figured he'd grow up to follow in his father's footsteps, be a mechanic or work in the coal mines, fingers worn down to the bone, and farm in his spare time for fun. *If farming is fun,* Blake often thought, *I'd rather be working.*

The truck roared to life, and a 15-minute drive stood between them and town.

"Okay, listen up you two," their mother said, as the truck rumbled down the rough two-lane. Her name was Patricia Kiser, but everybody called her Pat or Patty. Blake and Dianne called her 'mom,' of course. "I want both of you to pick out three or four good outfits. Nothing too expensive though. And Annie, you need some new shoes."

"I think I need some new shoes too, Mom," Blake said, eyeing the hole beginning to form at the toe of his right sneaker.

Kenneth S. Harris

"We can't really afford it right now, Blake." She looked down at his shoes and her eyes widened. "But we'll figure something out. Those are worn completely out!"

"They wouldn't be if I didn't have to work so much," Blake mumbled.

His mother eyed him disapprovingly. "Thank you, son," she said. "It's been a big help to us. You know we can't afford to pay anybody else to do it right now."

"I know," he said, ashamed. "I guess I shouldn't complain."

It was around 9 a.m. when they arrived at the Sun Rise Plaza, the only shopping center Hemingford had. There were four other cars in the parking lot.

Patty gave brief instructions for what she wanted Blake to find, then she and Dianne hurried off down towards *Watson's* to pick out clothes. The last thing she said was:

"Try not to go over 40 dollars honey."

First things first, Blake thought. *Shoes.*

He walked down the sidewalk to *Saving Soles,* the shoe store almost at the end of the plaza. Only Bachman's Pawn stood between *Saving Soles* and Hatton Street, where traffic was beginning to stir slightly.

Blake walked into the store. The front door was imprinted with a large white cross with gaudy rays of light protruding outward in an inexcusably trite attempt at 3-D. Below, in white letters: *Saving Soles, Where You May Save More than Money.* Blake rolled his eyes and entered.

The store seemed so big to him, filled with rows of shoes. Shoes were even lining the walls. Blake knew he couldn't afford a pair that he would actually want, so he

6

didn't bother to look. It seemed that the boys section was set up to where the prices got higher with each row running left to right, with the most expensive, and also the coolest, shoes being on the wall. He confined himself to the first two rows.

He picked out a pair of black and white sneakers, very ordinary, and sat down in the floor to try them on. They fit okay. His feet didn't seem to be getting any bigger. He took them off and put them back in the box, but before he could make his way to the front of the store to check out, he felt eyes on him.

"You really like those?" the girl said.

He turned around, faced with a young girl wearing black leggings, a multi-colored skirt that looked somewhere between tie-dye and a melted bag of *Skittles*, a brown tank top, one old green and white sneaker, and one new blue and white sneaker, the tag still dangling from the new shoe. She had a tangled series of bracelets on her wrists that looked like they ranged from gel bracelets to twisted-together bread-ties. Her brown hair was short and choppy and hung just above her shoulders. She seemed to be about his age.

"Yeah, they're okay," Blake said.

"Wouldn't you rather have some Nikes, or maybe Adidas?"

"What's it to you?" he scowled. "Say, aren't those boy's shoes?" he added, eyeing the blue and white sneaker on the girl's right foot. "Why would you try on boy's shoes? Cheap ones at that. 'Wouldn't you rather have the *Nikes?*'"

"One answer at a time," she said. "First of all, no. No Nikes for me. I like these much better. They're more

7

comfortable. Better for running, better for climbing, riding bikes, just about everything. And second, I like boy's shoes. It seems that every pair of girl's shoes that are my size has pink on them. I'm not really into pink."

"Odd," Blake said. "I thought all girls liked pink."

"I thought all boys wanted Nike or Adidas," she said matter-of-factly.

Blake walked over to the wall where the more expensive shoes sat on clear plastic pedestals, seeming to shimmer beneath the false light of the fluorescents overhead. He picked up a red and black Nike shoe.

"Eighty-nine bucks," he said, eyeing the price tag. "That's a lot of money. Why would anybody spend that kind of cash on shoes? They all wear the same, don't they? And just think of all the other stuff you could buy."

"Like what?" the girl said.

"I don't know. Anything. A new fishing pole, or candy bars. A few notebooks of paper."

"Interesting," she said. "But why the black and white?"

"Huh?"

"The shoes. The ones you're buying are just black and white. That's a little plain, don't ya think? And they match the pair you're wearing now."

"I like 'em just fine," Blake said, thinking that the girl thought way too much of her own opinion. Why else would she give it so frequently?

"I try to get a different color every time my mom makes me buy a new pair. I don't know why. I guess I just like colors!" She smiled, and in spite of himself, Blake found the smile to be sort of pretty. He shook his head and stifled a grin.

"I guess I don't mind things being plain," he said. "No offense, but you sort of look like you fell into a creek where a rainbow exploded."

She laughed. "What's wrong with that?"

Nothing, it's actually pretty cool, Blake thought, but he would never admit it.

"Whatever," he said. "You do what you like, and I'll stick to my black and whites. Deal?"

"Sure," she said. She looked like she was going to say more, but Blake walked off, heading towards the register, which was nestled in between a towering stack of religious pamphlets and another stack of pocket Bibles, each standing above a sign that said, *Free! Take one!*

Blake paid for his shoes quickly, nodding at every blessing and prayer the clerk offered and exited the store before the girl had even gotten the blue and white shoe off of her foot and back into the box. The total for his shoes was just a little over $15. His mom would be pleased.

The cashier had insisted he take one of the home-made pamphlets printed on sky-blue paper. It was a message about sinners and the Lord and the undeniable relationship between the two. Blake folded it and put it in his jeans pocket.

He quickly walked down the sidewalk to find his mother. He wasn't sure why, but he wondered if the girl was going to buy the blue and white shoes.

2

Blake and his family were home again before 3 o'clock, so there was plenty of time for him to finish his chores while Dianne tried on each of her new outfits and showed them to Dad. Blake ended up getting two new pairs of blue-jeans, two new T-shirts, and one gray button-up. He wasn't keeping count of how many outfits Dianne had gotten, but it took the better part of three hours for her to try them on.

Truth be told, Blake didn't really mind. He guessed girls needed more clothes than boys. He also thought that all girls liked pink, but apparently he was wrong.

Blake came into the house around 6 o'clock. When they had returned, Dad asked him to mow the grass around the farm, and all property included. It was a lot of grass to cut. His back was aching and he could still feel the hum of the old push mower clear up to his elbows. He was covered from head to foot in dirt and sweat and tiny flecks of chopped grass. Thin dark lines had started to form in the creases of his elbows and neck.

After a hot bath, he settled down in his room to work on a carving he'd started earlier in the week. It was a tiny replica of his family's old truck. It had slowly taken form out of a 3 inch chunk of birch Blake had sawed off a limb out by the back porch, bark giving way to the wood's white flesh, coming away in long strips at first, then smaller shavings and chips, until at last, detail. He had been too tired the previous evening, but he couldn't go two days in a row without doing something creative.

He turned the overhead light off, but left the lamp on beside his bed. He felt his way through the carving, rendering the fine details of the old Chevy with the tip of his worn, old Case pocket knife.

His parents were a divided force when it came to Blake's hobbies. He liked all sorts of creative activities: whittling, writing, drawing. Dad kept urging the boy towards chores and learning to fix cars, and felt that his craft only took time away from things that mattered. Mom, however, encouraged him greatly, just so long as Dad wasn't around.

He finished the carving quickly, seeing as how most of it was already completed. He then took out a pencil and paper and created a quick sketch of the cornfield as it looked outside his window under the blanket of night. This only took up the bottom half of the page, so he began to draw at the top, above the tall stalks of corn. He needed to be conservative with his paper. He was almost out.

His mind was wandering. School began again day after tomorrow. He wondered what his new teachers would be like, and if the classes would get any harder than they already were. Prominently, he wondered where the girl from the shoe store went to school, and if her classes began on Monday as well. He had never seen her around town before.

His mind often wandered as he created things. It was as close to meditation as he would ever come, he was sure of it. The one time his mind wasn't too busy to think.

Drawing, whittling, writing, they all came naturally. He didn't need to think about them. Therefore, he found time to think about other things while his hands crafted images that he kept deep inside his mind.

The image above the cornfield had started to take shape. He recognized her almost immediately, though he had not while he was drawing. It was the girl from the shoe store, a scratched out sketch, yet still recognizable, smiling her unusual smile that for some reason Blake couldn't seem to forget.

3

Blake felt surrounded by familiarity, standing at the end of his driveway in the early fog of a Monday morning, drowning in morning dew and déjà vu. Sunday was filled with church, God, and supper: a typical end of the week.

The air was chilly. School or no school, it was still summer and the air had no business being this cool. Unfortunately, Blake lived far enough from his school that the bus ran an hour and a half before the 8 o'clock bell rang. Dianne had it a bit easier this year. The bus that ran to the high school wouldn't arrive for another 45 minutes or so, since Hemingford High was so much closer than Nell Gilman Middle School.

The bus ride was always long and lonely. He had no friends on his bus. Actually, Blake didn't have many friends at all since Matt moved away. He shuddered at the thought of enduring a full year of school without Matt by his side. They'd had all the same classes since he started school, and just the five weeks he had suffered after Matt moved at the end of the last school year were just about enough to kill him. And to make matters worse, he and Van Dougherty had ridden the same bus since Blake was in first grade.

Van was an eighth-grader who should have been a tenth-grader. He didn't quite see the injustice of picking on kids much smaller and younger than him. He was probably the only middle-school kid who had fine stubble across his face, obviously proud to grow it, and long, sandy brown hair. He even had a driver's license, but the middle school had no place for students to park.

The calm of the morning was soon interrupted by the hum of the school bus jostling down Crystal Creek Road. The hum was constant, and seemed to be backing the chorus of crickets that had been singing solo.

It changed pitches for a moment, and Blake heard the hiss of the door opening. He looked down the road to see the bus sitting in the fog with each of its headlights glowing as Hayley Adams boarded. Hayley had lived a few houses down from Blake for years, but had hardly ever spoken to him. Then again, "a few houses down" was at least a quarter of a mile away and just barely visible in the early morning fog.

The bus started again, roaring towards him with its headlights carving a path through the dense white. It looked ghostly.

Blake waited patiently, but was surprised when the bus stopped again just briefly. The bus had stopped in front of the house just opposite the cornfield. *The new neighbors*, Blake thought, remembering the headlights from the other night.

He squinted to try to make out who it was, but couldn't tell. It was too dark and the fog was too thick.

The bus door opened again for Blake within seconds and he climbed aboard.

"G'mornin'," Irvin said.

Irvin Milhouse had been Blake's bus driver ever since he had started school. The kids all called him Swervin'

Irvin behind his back, but truthfully, Irvin was a hell of a guy. A tiny, old man with a balding head beneath his trucker cap who could never justify raising his voice.

Blake nodded and once again took in the familiarity of the situation. The bus smelled the same, like stale leather. A few kids sat sparsely about with sleepy eyes or their heads leaning against the windows. All except for one kid: the girl from the shoe store.

She sat wide-eyed about midways back, sitting with posture that was impressive for 6:30 in the morning. She had a red headband in her hair, pushing it back in front, and wore tiny black earrings. She waved to Blake excitedly when she saw him.

He sat down in the seat in front of her.

"You go to my school?" he said.

"It looks that way. I didn't know it was your school, though. How'd you get it? Win it in a lucky hand of stud?"

"Funny," Blake said, and started to move to another seat.

"Wait, wait, wait," the girl said. "It was just a joke. Relax, please. I'm Gretchen Wills, but everybody back home calls me Greta." She extended her hand.

Blake turned around and eyed the girl cautiously. He didn't normally open up to people, and he was used to being teased. Normally, he considered every scenario to have the potential to end badly. Regardless, he shook Greta's hand.

"I'm Blake Kiser."

"It's very nice to meet you," Greta said. "I'm a little nervous about meeting new people. It's my first day here. What are the other kids like? Are they cool?"

"Um, I guess they're okay," Blake said.

He could tell she didn't believe him by the way she looked at him.

"Okay," Blake conceded. "Most kids here are *not* cool."

He laughed, and she joined him.

"Let's just say I've not had much luck making friends," he said. He was into being honest, not interested in a herd of friends with wool over their eyes. The "cool" thing would have been to pretend like everyone was awesome, and that he had an endless number of friends. But for some reason, he had long ago grown tired of trying to be something he's not.

Plus, he felt that he didn't need to try to impress Greta. She didn't seem too concerned with "cool."

"You're doing fine," she said. "I think *we're* friends. So, it's only a few minutes into the first day of school, and we've both made a new friend. I'd call that a good thing. Or maybe just lucky." She laughed.

And again, Blake noticed her smile.

"Yeah, I'd like it if we were friends," he said. "You're probably the weirdest person I've ever met. And weird is sort of hard to come by in this town. Well, the good kind of weird anyway."

"Thanks," she said proudly. "I was hoping we'd be friends. I mean, we're neighbors whether we want to be or not."

"You mean?" Blake stammered, finally putting it all together. "You're family moved into the Johnston's old house?"

Greta nodded, still smiling.

"Cool," he said. "You know, every kid in these parts thinks that place is haunted. They're scared to death of it."

Greta seemed amused.

"I suppose they'll have to leave the haunted house stories to the old Bradley house at the head of Caine's Creek. Now that you've moved into the Johnston's old house, I mean."

"You mean there's more than one 'haunted' house around here?" she said.

"Yep. Pretty silly, huh?"

"I don't really believe in ghosts. But I don't disbelieve in them either. I just know that I've never seen one. So, I have no proof either way. Sort of like God."

"Careful who you say that around," Blake whispered, grinning in spite of himself. "Folks don't joke around about God."

"Duly noted," Greta said, nodding with closed eyes. "I didn't offend you, did I?"

"Nah," Blake said, waving it off. "Makes sense to me. You can't prove something you've never seen. All I know for sure about religion is I don't really care for church—all those folks acting the exact same way with hands in the air, waving around."

Greta laughed. "I rather like church, usually. It's so theatrical!"

They sat still for a moment and let silence settle.

"Well, I don't believe in ghosts. It just seems stupid," Blake said. "Not *real* ghosts anyway."

"Do you like ghost stories?" Greta asked.

"Yeah," he said. "You know any?"

"None that I could tell before we get to school. They take a pretty long time."

"It's an awful long trip," Blake said.

"We should get together after school one day and I'll tell a few. Ghost stories, crime stories, suspense, romance!"

"Romance?" Blake said. "I think I'll pass on that one."

Greta laughed. "Whatever you say," she said, rolling her eyes.

"I love to tell stories. It's one of my favorite things in the world. That and whittle."

"Whittle? What the hell is that?"

"You don't know what whittling is?" Blake couldn't believe his ears.

"If I did, I wouldn't have asked," Greta laughed.

"Whittling is like carving. Take a knife, and a chunk of wood, and make something cool out of it."

"You're allowed to play with knives?" She gave him a disapproving look.

"You have a lot to learn about Hemingford," Blake laughed.

The bus stopped, the door hissed open, and Van Dougherty stepped on board. He carried no backpack or school supplies—why would he? He would never use them—only a pack of smokes rolled tight in his shirt sleeve. He glowered at Blake as he walked by.

Greta looked at him in disbelief. "Does he carry one too?"

4

Blake was disappointed to learn that Greta was in a grade lower than him. She was a sixth grader, Blake a seventh. This was exceptionally unfortunate, seeing as how sixth graders and seventh graders weren't even in the same building.

The campus of the middle school was sectioned into two parts: a moderately large two-story building with seventh-grade classrooms on the first floor, eighth-grade classrooms on the second floor, and a cozy lunchroom in the basement; and a series of smaller buildings for the sixth graders that ran along both sides of a small wooden walkway with a tin roof.

Blake had put in his time in the tiny sixth-grade classrooms. He was moving up to bigger and better things. He wished Greta was with him though.

School proved to be everything he thought it would be. By lunchtime he had already managed to get scolded for drawing in class; he watched pretty girls in tiny shorts pretend he didn't exist; and he had managed to have a run-in with Van and Ronnie.

They'd caught him in the boy's restroom, which was strange and creepy enough to Blake even without their presence. It was oddly dark with no windows at all, lit only by dull artificial ceiling lights that seemed to make the shadows liquefy.

"Nice shoes," Van had said. "I bet your *Pa* had to save up right near all his chicken money to get you them, huh?" Van did not normally speak with such a country drawl as he was using when he spoke to Blake.

"You know," Ronnie chimed in with similar country slang, though his wasn't intentional. "Spending all his time with his daddy's chickens, it ain't no wonder he's turned into one himself."

Van and Ronnie both had a good laugh as Blake tried to get around them and out of the boy's room. However, Ronnie held Blake down while Van wrote the word "loozer" across the toe on both of his new shoes.

When lunchtime rolled around, Blake hurried to the cafeteria and got his food quickly. He was sitting in a back corner of the basement lunchroom eating alone, when he heard a familiar voice from across the rickety wooden lunch table.

"Hey buddy," Greta said. "We got the same lunch period!"

She looked different in the light of the lunchroom than she had in the darkness of the bus that morning. Each color of her outfit seemed more vibrant. She wore black pants and a black T-shirt with a bright blue tank-top over top of it, red belt and red headband.

"Thank God!" Blake said with relief. "Today's been crazy. It's about time I get some good news."

"Crazy day, huh? Do tell."

Blake lifted one of his shoes up onto the table so that Greta could read the word Van Dougherty had misspelled on the white toe of his black and white sneakers.

"How'd that happen?" Greta said, the look on her face mingling between disbelief and anger. "Your new shoes!"

"Remember the big, creepy guy on the bus this morning? Him and his buddy Ronnie," Blake said. "They've been picking on me ever since first grade. Actually, I don't think it's anything personal. They pick on everybody now that I think about it."

"You mean to tell me that guy goes here? To middle school?"

"Yeah, he's been held back more times than he can probably count."

"That still gives him no right to do this," she said, gesturing at Blake's ruined sneakers. "Somebody should kick his ass!"

"I would," Blake said. "But they're both bigger than me. Next time I'll buy shoes that are all black."

"What kind of a solution is that, kid?" Greta asked.

"Hey, sixth grader! Who you calling 'kid?'"

They both laughed.

"No, what I mean is you shouldn't have to change to avoid assholes," Greta said. "What if you buy black shoes, shoes you didn't really want, and they just use White-Out to write hideously misspelled words on them?" She sighed, exasperated. "You should buy the shoes you want, and protect them!"

"Easier said than done," Blake said. "Maybe one day they'll get what's coming to 'em. One way or another. Maybe they won't. Anyway, how are you liking it here so far?"

The lunchroom was full now and the buzz of chatter would rattle the head of anyone not used to the sound. A visitor to the school could probably feel their brain bouncing off one side of their skull and then the other, being shook by the roar of dozens of children confined to a small underground space.

"It's pretty cool," she said. "The classes are easy enough. The teachers seem okay. It *is* hard to make friends here, though. Every time I try talking to someone they just snicker and look away, or ignore me altogether. But I guess I don't really have the right to complain when my new best friend is getting "loozer" wrote on his brand new shoes."

Best friend! The term rang in Blake's head. He hadn't had a best friend since Matt left, not even a self-proclaimed one.

"I'm not worried about it," Blake said, trying to hide his bashfulness. "With enough elbow grease anything will come out. I'll just have to work at it."

"Elbow grease?" Greta said, confused. "What's that?"

"Really? It's just a saying for working hard," Blake said. He kept forgetting she wasn't from Hemingford. Did that make her weird? Yes, of course! That amongst other things.

"I see," she said. She looked confused.

"You'll get the hang of it," Blake said, smiling. "Where was it you said you were from?"

"Connecticut," Greta said. "Little place called Greenwich."

Lunch was over far too quickly. Blake and Greta had been so heavily immersed in conversation they barely had time to eat. They parted ways at the lunchroom exit, Blake heading up the stairs to the seventh-grade classrooms,

Greta heading across the school's parking lot towards the sixth-grade buildings.

Blake watched her walk for a moment, along with all the other sixth graders. Most walked in clusters and groups of four or five, laughing, talking, horse-playing. Greta walked alone. She reminded him of himself the previous year. However, it was only her first day here. She would probably be swarming with friends in a week or two.

He looked down at his shoes, not sure if all the elbow grease in the world would do the trick. Then he remembered the black and red Nikes from the shoe store. *"Loozer" wouldn't show up on the black toe of those sneakers*, he thought. *That's probably why they were more expensive.*

5

That evening Blake and Greta met in front of the corn-field where Blake had spent most of his summer days. On the bus ride home they had planned to meet up and tell ghost stories, inspired by the old house at the head of Caine's Creek.

Greta went first. As they walked the roadway away from their homes, she told him a tale of kids who were ghosts but didn't know it. They'd lived in their house day after day, and their mother would never let them leave. The end of the story revealed the children to be ghosts anchored to earth by their mothers love for them, and her inability to cope with their passing. She let them go in the end and their spirits soared away into the sky into an intriguingly better unknown. The end.

"That was pretty cool," Blake said. "Where you learn stories like that?"

He scuffed his feet against the dusty road as they walked.

"My dad used to tell me stories before bed every night," she said. "I loved every story he would tell. He doesn't do it so much anymore. But every now and then, he'll slip into my room after the lights are already out and tell me a story with just the nightlight on."

Greta gasped at the slip of the word "nightlight." Blake paid it no mind.

"I like to write stories down," Blake said. "My parents never told me bedtime stories, not even when I was really little. I wish they would've though. It sounds pretty cool. Guess I'm getting too old for it now."

"It is cool," Greta said, watching her feet as she walked. "And you're never too old to hear a good story. Are you going to tell me one?"

"I can tell you the one about that old house on Caine's Creek," he said. "You know, 'Hemingford's haunted house, number two.'"

"Sure. Go for it."

"It goes like this," Blake began. "A long time ago, way before I was even born, an old man, Mr. Bradley, lived there by himself. His wife was dead. He had two kids, but his daughter died when she was little, drowned in the pond up on Caine's Creek. It's up the hill a little ways. Everybody who lives up there likes to fish in it. But nobody was fishing that day. And his son moved to New York to become a doctor or somethin' like that.

"Anyway, some folks say that the old man went insane up there. Insane from the pain of losing his family. Insane from the boredom, from being alone. Nobody really knows for sure. They say he kept talking about seeing his daughter at night, even though she was dead. Eventually, he hung himself out in the backyard of that old house from a tree that's been standing there for centuries. He was drove to it by the ghost of his daughter. Or that's how the story goes anyway. And now, folks say that his ghost haunts that old house, and anybody that goes in it will never come out again."

Greta wasn't speaking, even though the story had ended. She stared at Blake as though waiting for him to finish. Her eyes were wide and her mouth hung slightly open. Blake thought she looked scared, but wouldn't dare call her on it.

To his surprise, Greta said, "Can we see it?"

"See what?" Blake was confused. "You mean?"

"The house!" Greta trilled. "I bet it's awesome!"

They had lost track of the time and the place. They had ventured farther from home than they had intended to, almost to the mouth of Crystal Creek, and would have to return home in the dark. Currently, Greta didn't seem to mind. Her eyes glistened with excitement as she bounded about, trumping Blake's joy from earlier in the evening.

"You want to go ... You want to see that old house? Why on earth would you want to do a thing like that?"

"Oh, come on!" she said. "You don't really believe all that do you? First of all, there are no ghosts. Period. Well, I don't think," she grinned. "Anyway, you don't even believe in them, remember? And even if there were, I don't think they would want to hurt anybody!"

"Yeah? First of all, I don't believe in ghosts. But that old house is just creepy, and probably dangerous. But if that story *is* true, the ghost of that little girl drove the old man to kill himself!" Blake swallowed hard. "I don't want to go out like that!"

Greta laughed. "Come on! Won't you show it to me?" She smiled and clasped both hands beneath her chin. "Please!"

Blake shuffled his feet against the dry dirt that covered the road. He looked everywhere but into Greta's eyes. When he could no longer avoid that electric-blue-eyed stare, reluctantly, he said, "Okay, but not tonight. It's getting dark, there's school tomorrow, and it's a long hike."

"How about this weekend?" Greta asked.

Blake couldn't believe he was about to agree to this. The Bradley house. He'd heard so many stories about that place, and had even seen it a couple of times. He and Matt had visited last Halloween just for kicks and had ended up getting spooked and running clear to the mouth of Caine's Creek. He had to be braver than that around Greta.

"Okay," he said. "But you owe me. Big time."

6

The week passed quickly enough. School offered more of the same negatives for Blake and Greta, but they were adjusting. Greta seemed to like her English teacher, Ms. O'Connor, a lot better than the one she had back in Greenwich. Blake wasn't surprised by this; he thought highly of Ms. O'Connor as well.

By the time school ended on Friday, Greta was about to bust with excitement. Blake, however, could think of better ways to spend his weekend than by going to see the Bradley house, but he knew there would be no talking her out of it.

"Okay," Blake said loudly, trying to speak over the vocal clutter of the other children as the bus drew ever closer home. "Meet me early in the morning. We'll get an early start, and try to be back before it gets dark."

"How early?" Greta asked.

"Around eight."

Greta looked shocked.

"I told you it was a long walk," Blake said.

"No, it's not the early start that bugs me," she said. "And it's sure not the walk. But it's a 'haunted house,' right? Wouldn't it only be fitting to see it after dark?"

"After dark? No way!" Blake said. "My mom would skin me if I was out that late!"

"You're just afraid," Greta said matter-of-factly.

Blake sighed. He knew he wasn't getting out of this one.

"I'll make a deal with you," he said. "Dusk. That way it ain't quite dark yet, but it ain't daytime either. What do you say?"

Greta thought about it for a moment, looking unnecessarily pensive.

"If that's the best you can do, I suppose dusk will be okay," she said. "But I want to see the tree too."

"The tree?"

"The tree where the old man hung himself."

"Are you secretly some kind of psychopath? Or a sick-o?" Blake asked, grinning and squinting at her. "Why would you want to see something like that?"

"One answer at a time," she said. "First, I am not a psycho! Or a sick-o! You should know me better than that! Second, I would want to see the tree to prove that there is nothing *creepy* about it. It's still just a tree! It's part of nature. It's not evil."

Blake snickered to himself and eyed his thumbs, fumbling about in his lap.

"What is it?" Greta asked. "What's so funny?"

"Oh nothing," he said. "It's just that you have to be the only person on this planet that would ever want to see that tree. Most kids won't even look at the house very long. You want to walk right past it and into the backyard." He smiled. "If there *is* a ghost, we're screwed."

Out of nowhere, a damp wad of paper stuck to the side of Greta's face. A trickle of saliva gushed from it upon impact. She picked it off and looked at it disgusted. Blake heard Van's familiar laugh coming from behind him. He turned to glare at Van, who sat with his back to the window, legs lax in the seat, filthy hunting boots dangling over the edge.

Blake was furious but he didn't know what to do or say.

Greta glared at him and said in a steady voice, "Ass. Hole. What the hell is your problem?"

Van's smile broadened. "That's gutsy, you little bitch. I just thought a nice wet one would look good with that ridiculous outfit."

Greta looked down at her outfit, then back to Van. She was wearing blue-jean shorts over top of black mesh leggings and a yellow V-neck T-shirt, snug to her form. Blake found all he could do was watch.

"This outfit? No, not really. This disgusting piece of shit doesn't go with it at all." She tossed the spit wad back in Van's direction. "But then again, how would I expect you to know that? How many times have you been held back? Four? Five?"

Shit, Blake thought.

The smile faded from Van's face. He rose up in the seat and propped his elbows on the backs of his seat and the seat in front of him.

"Maybe nobody told you yet, but do *not* fuck with me. Talk to me like that again, and you *will* regret it." Van was so close to them, Blake could almost feel his breath on his face, coming out in hot gusts that reeked of cigarette smoke.

Greta laughed. "That's almost believable," she said. "But let me make this clear. You do *not* scare me at all."

Van lunged to his feet. "Then you're dumber than you look."

Before he knew what he was doing, Blake was standing in the aisle between Van and Greta.

"What the fuck?" Van said. "When did you grow a pair, *loser*?"

"Just leave her alone," Blake said, meekly.

Van snarled and grabbed Blake's shirt. Irvin must have noticed. Blake heard a loud bang, familiar, but just barely—Irvin didn't do this often. He didn't need to. Blake saw Irvin brandishing a large, flat board, having just finished slapping the front of the bus with it several times. The sound echoed throughout the enclosed space, but when it stopped, the roar of children had become silent. Even Van had winced and turned to face the front of the bus.

"What's the problem back there, boys?" Irvin said, his voice hushed in comparison to the loud rap of the wood on the bus' metal interior. He glanced up into the rearview mirror to look at them, but just for a moment.

"No problem," Van said. "Just getting to know the new girl."

"I see," Irvin said. "Well, it looks like you're doing a bad job of it. Sit down."

Van didn't say anything, but backed into his seat, plopping down with a thud against the cracked leather. Blake remained standing, but just for a moment. His hands were shaking uncontrollably, so he stuffed them into his pockets before taking his seat next to Greta.

"It's cool," she said. "All good."

"Yeah, I guess so," Blake said. "I just can't believe you did that. Nobody that I know of has ever stood up to him like that."

"Well, this is one girl he's not going to pick on." She smiled and for a moment Blake felt reassured, though it didn't last long. When they stood to exit the bus, Blake noticed Van's glare never left Greta, not even as they stood in her driveway and the bus drove away.

***

Blake was awake and packed for their journey by 7:30 the next morning. The sun hadn't risen completely yet as he left the house to meet Greta in front of the corn field, and neither had his parents.

Blake had done extra chores the previous evening, and had told his parents he was going to show his new friend around town, and maybe even show her around the woods where he and Matt used to play.

He put on a pair of blue jeans and a faded red T-shirt. His battered baseball cap completed his outfit. But strangely, it had never seen a game of baseball.

Greta was nowhere in sight when Blake arrived at the cornfield. He sat down in front of the towering stalks and waited patiently. He had only been waiting for a few seconds when he heard a noise. It was a ghostly noise, fitting for the day: a soothing note, pitched high and set to waver. He sat perfectly still and listened. He wasn't afraid to move, surely not. But moving would create noise and make the noise harder to hear.

He was trying to make up his mind whether or not to turn around to investigate, when a pair of hands grabbed his shoulders and pulled him back into the corn. The ghostly noise rose higher and louder until it dissolved into the sound of Greta laughing.

"Not funny!" Blake said. "Why'd you do that? You're gonna wake up my parents."

"Shhh!" she said. "No, I'm not. They're all the way back at the house. Besides, I just thought it was a good way to start the day."

"If you say so."

"I do!" She smiled broadly, exposing pearly white teeth.

Blake couldn't help but chuckle a bit too.

Greta was wearing blue-jean shorts and a green-plaid buttoned shirt over a white T-shirt, along with her blue and white shoes.

"Okay, inventory check before we leave," Blake said. He picked up the backpack that had earlier in the week held each and every one of his school books. The concept of having a locker was still new to him and he had yet to use it. But last night he had spilled out all the books and school supplies and filled it with supplies for the road.

"I've got two sandwiches for each of us and a bag of potato chips. I got a flashlight in case it gets too dark on the way back. And that's about it. How about you?"

"I took my dad's canteen and filled it with water. I don't think he'll miss it unless he and mom plan a last minute camping trip without me. I brought two candy bars, some crackers, rope, a watch, some paper and a few pencils."

Blake raised his eyebrows.

"We may get bored," she clarified.

"Okay. It looks like we're all set. Let's get going."

When the two of them set off towards Caine's Creek the sun was finally rising in the eastern sky. They found themselves walking into an exploding sunrise. Blake thought Greta deserved that sky; they seemed to have the same personality.

Crystal Creek took them to the two-lane road that would eventually lead to town if traveled southward. Blake and Greta, however, traveled it north, towards the turn-off for Caine's Creek.

It was only a matter of minutes before the sun felt hot enough to blister. They wiped sweat on their shirt sleeves and kicked up dry dust as if to signify just how hot the day really was. Blake picked up a thick tree branch that had fallen by the roadside from one of the lush maples that lined the bank. He clanked it rhythmically against the dry ground as they walked.

"So, you ended up buying those blue shoes after all," Blake said, after a few moments silence.

"Yep," Greta said. "I had to have 'em."

"How come I haven't seen you wearing them at school?"

"Blake Kiser, have you been staring at my feet at school?" she laughed. "Are *you* some kind of sick-o?"

"No!" Blake said, laughing as well. "It's just, well, those are some bright shoes. I think I'd notice if someone was wearing a pair that look like that."

He pointed to her toes, where she displayed the blue and white shoes playfully. Being layered by dust, the *new* of Greta's new shoes was quickly wearing thin. No matter, she seemed as proud of them as ever, if not more so. Blake tucked his toes inward trying to hide "loozer," which he had scrubbed to no worthy end. He had even considered going over them with a marker of his own.

Greta informed Blake that it was after 1 o'clock when they sat down to eat lunch. They found a spot off of the main road on the bank of a broad, flowing creek. Blake sat on a large flat rock that overlooked the water; Greta plopped down right in the sand.

Blake was a little concerned that they hadn't made very good time. He had expected them to be much further along than this by now, but talking to Greta seemed to distract. He was thinking more about the journey than the destination.

"Me and my friend Matt used to fish here," Blake said through a mouthful of peanut butter. "Never really caught anything. I don't think there's a fish in this whole creek. Now, Caine's Creek, that's a different story! There's a lot of good places to fish up there."

"I used to go fishing with my dad. But it's been a while since he's had enough free time to take me," Greta said. "Who's Matt?"

"Matt was my best friend," Blake said. "We were in all the same classes since kindergarten."

"What happened to him?"

"He died in that old house we're going to see."

Greta paused mid-bite and shot Blake an incredulous glare.

"Just messing with you," Blake laughed. "He moved away. Pennsylvania, I believe it was. We said we'd keep in touch, but it's been almost four months and we haven't really."

Greta took another bite of her sandwich.

"I guess that's how friends are though," Blake said. "If there is anything I've learned from school and life in general, it's that every friend always leaves you in the end."

"What about your mom and dad," Greta said, after a moment's silence. "They're still with each other, and they've gotta be friends to be married, right?"

"I reckon married people are a special kind of friends," Blake said. "I mean, if they really want to be married, if they love each other and everything. Those kinds of friends seem to stick everything out. Probably because there's nothing else that's more important. I guess they figure everything will be alright if they just stick together. And for the most part they're right, I guess."

"For the most part?" Greta inquired.

"Yeah, mistakes happen, I suppose," Blake snickered. "I mean, after all, my parents had Dianne didn't they?"

***

Their legs were starting to get sore when they turned onto Caine's Creek. It was a little after 3 o'clock, and the August sun was still blazing. Greta had taken her plaid over-shirt off and tied it around her waist, and her white T-shirt was already streaked with traces of dirt and dust.

"How can they even call this a road?" Greta asked, as they made their way down the tiny roadway, barely big enough for an automobile.

Blake laughed. "I don't know. I guess people around here are just used to it."

The road snaked away from them into the darkness created by overcast trees, reaching out high above the roadway with branches that strived to touch each other like longing fingertips. The sun was furiously hot, but Blake knew that in a few minutes they would be delivered into waiting shade. Caine's Creek was a haven for shade, a blessing on a hot day, but drearily damp for at about a week after a good rain.

Just before reaching the shade, they took turns sipping from the canteen. The water was still reasonably cool and felt soothing against their parched throats.

"Care to rest a while?" Greta asked once the shade was well overhead.

"A short while, maybe," Blake said. "We need to keep going if we're going to make it by the time the sun goes down."

"Okay," she said. "Just a minute."

Greta sat down on the side of the road letting her legs dangle above a very small, trickling creek. It was a high bank that held the roadway, and her feet were still at least a foot above the water. Blake joined her.

"It feels nice here, doesn't it?" she said.

"Yeah, nice on a hot day. Boy, it sure gets cold in the wintertime though. Colder than where we live, even though it's just a few miles away, if you can believe it."

It felt nice to be more knowledgeable than Greta about something, even if it was only his indigenous terrain.

"How much further is the house?" Greta asked.

"Hmm, about another mile or so."

"Did you say you and Matt used to come up this way? To the house, I mean," she said.

Blake couldn't speak at first, just stared at her for a moment. He hadn't talked about Matt in a long time. And already, he'd come up multiple times in one day.

"Yeah," Blake said. "We went to the house one Halloween on a bet. Ran out of here scared stiff." He laughed at how stupid they must have looked, dressed in the height of Halloween fashion, grocery bags bulging with candy dangling at their sides, running and screaming as though hell itself were on their heels. "But we used to come up here fishing all the time."

"Fishing? In that little creek?"

"No, there's a big pond a little way from here. It's off the main road. It's where the man's daughter drowned, remember?"

She nodded. "Oh yeah! Being here makes that story seem so much more real. Normally, when I hear something, it's just a story, even if it's true. But being here puts me in the story and lets me see it."

"You're so weird," Blake laughed.

"So are you!" Greta said, mocking his voice. "Not much we can do about it, though."

"I guess you're right. Let's get moving. I do *not* want to be here when it gets dark."

7

The sun was still up when Blake and Greta reached their destination. The house stood in the shade of the surrounding mountains and trees that formed the end of the hollow. The ground was plush with a thick moss in most places. It cushioned their footfalls like thick carpet over wooden floorboards.

The old house, all the paint faded and peeling from the weathered wood, looked like it was ready to fall apart. Every board, safe to say, was rickety.

"There you go," Blake said. "What do you think?"

"I can see why everybody thinks it's haunted," she said. "It has that look to it doesn't it?"

"To say the least."

"Just imagine, this was once somebody's home. Someone used to live here."

"Yeah, and then he lost his mind and hung himself," Blake said. "Can we go now?"

Greta shook her head energetically. "No way! The tree! You promised! And it's not dark yet. Come on!"

She entered the yard through a cracked and broken gate. The hinges were rusted and loose, allowing the gate to scrape the ground as it swung regretfully open. Grass engulfed a set of stone steps which bore the initial steep incline of the yard, ending in an overgrown cobblestone walkway which led to the front porch across the unkempt landscape. Blake imagined a blanket of snakes beneath the swaying tips of the towering grass.

Before Greta reached the porch, she strayed from the stones and trotted through the overgrown grass and around the side of the house. Blake reluctantly followed, imagining the tree hideous and gnarled with the hanging rope still dangling from it.

The tree stood apart from the rest. It was the only one inside the fragile fence, and was nowhere near gnarled. It stood large and proud, a tribute to years past, shading the back yard with large branches sprinkled with lush summer leaves. On one of the lower branches a tire swing hung, swaying softly in the breeze. Another low branch reached out from the mighty trunk, a sturdy arm to hold another swing, or to build a tree house upon, or ...

Blake remembered why they had come to see that tree, and suddenly realized that the branch must be the one that held the noose. It was the only one low enough. He could almost picture the man swaying in the same gentle breeze as the tire swing, each hanging limp at opposite ends of the sturdy trunk.

"There it is," Blake said. "You happy?"

Greta didn't answer, but instead ran to the tire swing and jumped inside. Blake gasped, thinking the old rotted rope holding the swing would break for sure. But it didn't, and Greta laughed gleefully as the swing sent her round about in large circles.

The image was so beautiful that all thoughts of nooses and hanging were swept from Blake's head. He ran to her side and gave her a push when the swing started to slow.

"You see?" Greta said. "There's nothing scary about it! This is wonderful! This tree is just as beautiful as any other on this planet!"

The children played for a while, taking turns and even trying to fit on the swing at the same time. It ended with Blake falling off of the swing, but laughing wildly as he hit the ground.

He had resumed pushing Greta in the swing when they both noticed the sun was gone. Dusk had almost turned to night, and they would surely have to walk out of Caine's Creek in the pitch dark. However, in spite of the jolting fear of what lie ahead, Blake couldn't help thinking how romantic it was to push Greta in the old swing. "Romantic." The word sounded so foreign to him, even in his thoughts.

"We should probably go," Greta said, hopping from the swing and dusting off the seat of her shorts.

"Yeah, it's gonna be dark," Blake said. "You're not scared are you?"

"Of course I'm not scared," Greta said.

"I am," he laughed. "But only of what mom and dad will do to me if they catch me sneaking in late at night."

She grabbed Blake's hand and they started walking back around the corner of the house. "No stopping to rest on the way back! That'll save some time."

"Deal."

She's holding my hand! entered Blake's mind, but vanished quickly. A large figure was standing on the back stoop watching them. Blake rubbed his eyes, thinking it was just shadows playing tricks on him.

But then, the thing from the shadows spoke.

"It's been a while since anybody's been messing around out here," the figure said. The voice was deep and gruff, roaring in the silence of the deserted back yard. "What are you kids doin'?"

For a moment, the two children stood voiceless in the gathering dark. They still held hands, both gripping a little tighter than before. It was Blake who spoke first.

"We just ... We just wanted to see the tree," he stammered.

"That old thing?" the man asked gruffly. "Why?"

"Is it your tree?" Greta asked. Blake wondered what she meant by that, wondered if she thought this man was a ghost, the true ghost of the old man who had hung himself here so many years ago. Only this man wasn't that old. And he didn't look anything at all like a ghost; at least not what Blake would have imagined a ghost to look like.

The man rubbed his chin, covered with a stubbly brown beard that matched his shaggy brown hair, as if deep in thought.

"You kids look bright," he said. "So, I won't even try to lie to ya. This ain't my house. And that ain't my tree. Yet. I'm thinking about buying the old place."

"If you plan to buy this place, you sure got a lot of work to do. If you haven't bought it yet, why are you living here?" Blake said, realizing how bold the question was only after asking it.

"Well, I'll be honest about that too. I need a place to stay for a while. And this place don't have nobody livin' in it. It seems to work out, don't it?"

Blake and Greta looked at each other. Blake shrugged. As far as he knew, no one had ever lived in this old house, not since the old man died.

"I don't see why anybody would want this place," Blake said.

"Why don't you two come on in? I'll show you around."

"No thanks," Blake said, without hesitation. He had picked up enough common sense from his family to know that going into an abandoned house with a stranger is never a good idea.

"Isn't that why you two came up here?" the man asked. "Let me guess! Every kid in these parts thinks this place is haunted?" His eyes were now large and bright. He was grinning devilishly.

"That's right," Greta said. "And we did come to see the house. Well, more the tree than the house really. But yeah, to make a long story short: we, I mean, *I* wanted to see a haunted house."

"Well come on in and see it," the man said.

"Just the same, no thanks," Blake said.

"I see. I see," the man said. "Lack of trust. And I don't blame you. You don't know me. For that matter, I don't know you either. So I understand."

Blake and Greta glanced at each other inquisitively. They seemed to be conversing with the terrified looks in their eyes. Blake was afraid for Greta, and to be honest, for himself as well. He had heard stories of strangers stealing children, and the children were never seen again except in black and white photographs on fliers at local department stores and on milk cartons.

But at the same time, he didn't want to anger the man. He supposed as long as they kept their distance they would be okay.

"I didn't think anybody would ever live here," Blake said, more to himself than to the stranger. "How long have you been staying here? Where's your family?"

"Oh, for a couple of months," the man said. "I ain't got no family, really. At least, none that I care about. I sneak around and scrounge for food every now and then. I'll kill me a rabbit when I can and cook it over the fireplace. Sometimes a squirrel. I'll even dig around in garbage cans out behind grocery stores and stuff like that if I have to."

"You eat stuff that comes out of a garbage dump?" Greta asked, screwing up her face in a contorted grimace.

"When I have to," the man said.

Greta made a gagging noise. Blake motioned for her to stop for fear of angering the man. His face maintained the same expression, however. It was almost blank. But Blake thought he detected a notion of annoyance on the man's face towards the two children who had interrupted his pleasant evening, and furthermore, had discovered his living arrangement.

"Hey, I have to eat, don't I? I didn't say I liked it."

To Blake's relief, the man's mouth had cracked open in a natural toothy smile; not the whitest of smiles, but at least he had all of his teeth as far as he could tell.

"I guess so," Greta said. "What's your name?"

"I'm Cass. Cass Blighly. Most of my friends just call me Tex." He extended his hand to Blake and Greta, but neither of them moved to shake it, at least not at first. After a moment, Greta stepped forward and shook his hand. Reluctantly, Blake did the same.

"Blake Kiser," Blake said.

"I'm Gretchen Wills. Friends call me Greta. Why do they call you Tex? Are you from Texas?"

"Nope, I'm from Virginia," Cass said with a stern face. Then he snickered, which eventually spawned a fit of laughter. "I'm just playing," he said. "Nobody calls me Tex. Just a joke. You can call me Cass. At least for now. But don't make a habit of calling me anything."

"Same here," Blake said, somewhat apprehensively.

"How bout I make a deal with ya," Cass said.

"What kind of deal?" asked Blake.

"I won't tell your folks that you two were in my backyard swingin' on that swing, if you two won't tell anybody that I moved in. I just like my privacy, that's all. How's that sound?"

"Sounds fair enough to me," Greta said. "You think maybe we could come back some time and swing again?"

"No!" Cass said. "I normally don't take too well to people. They get on my nerves. *Especially* kids. Let's just stick to 'I won't tell, if you won't tell.'"

"Fair enough, I suppose," Greta said, hanging her head. She started to speak again, as if to protest either Cass's decision or his attitude, but Blake squeezed her hand to catch her attention. He shook his head slightly; *no, this is a bad idea, please don't make him angry.*

The sky had turned black as they stood talking, but suddenly it turned brilliant white as if it had caught fire for just a moment. Thunder followed, filling up the silence. Slowly, steadily, it began to rain.

"Oh no!" Blake said. "We have to walk home in this."

"We better get going," Greta said. "My parents won't like me being out in the rain, much less too late after dark. It was nice to have met you Cass. I don't guess we'll be seeing you again."

Cass waved them away with a large, dismissive hand and went inside the house.

"What do you make of that guy?" Blake asked now that he and Greta were alone once again in the back yard.

"I don't really know," Greta said. "But did you see the way he was always looking around? Looking at the trees, looking at the ground. Looking at almost anything except either one of us."

"Yeah, so what?"

"Well, I used to have a cousin back in Greenwich that did that. He was a compulsive liar. Never could look me in the eye."

"You think he's hiding something?" Blake asked.

"Not really hiding something," Greta said. "But not being completely honest, either. I think he's trying a little too hard to push us away because he doesn't want any friends. Maybe he has a tragic past, full of loss and sadness," she said in a mock fainting voice, laying one hand across her brow which was beaded with rain droplets—the perfect false swoon.

Blake laughed.

"Maybe that is what he wants," he said. "And guess what? He gets it. I don't want to be his friend. Now let's get out of here before we get drenched!"

"Well, he won't get rid of me so easily," Greta said.

Blake's mouth dropped. He couldn't believe what she was saying. He sighed heavily.

"Everybody needs friends, Blake!" she said. "Even you! Even Cass Blighly!"

"Greta, no! That's crazy. This guy could be dangerous. Use your head."

"Well, you'll just have to stick around to protect me then," she said followed by a muffled snicker. "Besides we'll only come back during the day. And if he was going to hurt us, he just had the perfect chance."

Blake sighed as they walked around the corner of the house, which stood in deeper darkness because of the tress. He knew that "he won't get rid of *me* so easily" roughly translated to "he won't get rid of *us* so easily." He wouldn't let Greta be around this man alone.

"I still say that guy is no good."

When they reached the front yard they saw a light gleaming on the porch. It was shining towards them, brighter than a flame.

"What's that?" Greta asked.

"I'm not sure."

He began walking towards it. Greta took his hand once again and followed. They walked slowly, the tall grass brushing long, wet streaks across their legs, until they reached the source of the light.

Sitting in a broken down rocking chair was a long handled flashlight on top of a folded parka, still in a plastic package. Beside these items was a note scribbled in terrible penmanship, almost illegible. It said:

Kenneth S. Harris

You can borrow these. But I want them back.
- Cass

It was a long journey home, and neither of them talked very much. Blake was too busy thinking about Cass. After all, "I want them back" meant that they had to make another trip to the head of Caine's Creek. They huddled tightly together, sharing the parka, as a downpour battered their heads and backs, occasionally blowing into their eyes.

It was black as pitch when they saw the cornfield on Blake's family's farm, the moon hiding behind the dark clouds in the sky. The tips of the stalks were growing up out of a gathering fog like soggy weeds in a murky swamp.

"I'll see you tomorrow," Greta said. "That is if my parents don't kill me."

"Same here," Blake said. He stayed out late all the time when Matt had lived in Hemingford, and his parents typically turned in around 9, assuming he would be home shortly. He supposed everything would be okay, depending on how late it actually was, and whether or not someone had looked into his room on a late-night trip to the bathroom.

"Good night," Greta said, and hugged him. "I had a really good time today. Even if it was a little creepy. But hey! What were we expecting, if not creepy? Going to see a haunted house and all." She smiled the beautiful smile that Blake was becoming so accustomed to.

"Good night," Blake said. "I hope you don't get in too much trouble."

She handed Blake the flashlight, but he insisted she keep it and the parka. "Just make sure your folks don't see them. They'll probably wonder where you got them."

They parted ways. As Blake walked up the driveway to the farm, he could see he was right: all the lights in the house were off. His parents and Dianne were asleep and the night was perfectly still. He only hoped the lights were off in Greta's house too.

He snuck around the side of the house, and with the assistance of a tired old maple tree, ascended the side of the porch, crossed the slippery overhang, and crept through his window that he seldom locked. For just a moment, he panicked when the window wouldn't budge, but then it gave way with a rattling jolt and slid up to allow him entry. He crept in and was asleep in minutes, leaving his soaking wet clothes and shoes on the floor. The last thing he acknowledged, just faintly, before tumbling into sleep was his shoes: "loozer" was beginning to fade away.

8

The next morning arrived so quickly, Blake felt as though he hadn't slept at all. The sun was bright and the rain from the previous night's storm was dissipating fast.

He hurried through his breakfast and worried his way through church. Out of all the random Sundays, his parents had to pick this one to actually *go* to church. His mom went often, but his dad typically liked to catch up on his sleep on Sundays. This rarity, when they had decided to go together and demand the presence of their children, could not have come on a more ill-timed day. Blake was exhausted. He was worried about how much trouble Greta was in. Dianne commented on the circles under his eyes.

When they returned home, Blake changed out of his church clothes and ran outside. His parents didn't want him to do chores on Sunday, so he just rambled about after church in the drying mud hoping that Greta would come outside and tell him that everything was fine and that she had not gotten into any trouble at all. But somehow, he doubted that.

After about 30 minutes or so of walking aimlessly about the farm, Blake could no longer stand the anticipation. He decided to pay a visit and knock on the Wills' door. He knew that if Greta was grounded or something, he would be extremely lonely; in fact, as lonely as he was a couple of weeks ago before he knew her. But also, it meant that he would have to return Cass's things by himself. Both reasons left him shivering.

He stepped up onto the porch and knocked meekly on the door. The porch was large and tidy, but with very little furniture, only an elongated swing built for two at the upper end. The house, in fact, looked much nicer close up than it did from the road or from his house. He marveled at the wide trim that surrounded the windows and door, coated with a fine pastel blue paint. The door was large with a brass knocker centered on it. The white painted siding was a little worn, but nothing that couldn't be fixed in time.

He waited for about a minute, and then knocked again.

Still no answer.

He felt odd standing on the porch of the old house that he'd looked at for years but had never been in. Apparently, Greta's parents weren't home, or she was in so much trouble that they wouldn't even bother answering the door.

He looked at the sky. It had to be getting close to 3 o'clock, or at least 2. He decided to go home.

As he walked down the porch steps, a shiny black car pulled into the driveway. It was a newer model sedan, around a '95 or '96 model. The windows were slightly tinted. The rear passenger's door opened and Greta got out smiling and waving.

"Hey Blake!" she said, as though nothing was wrong. "How are you this morn ... well, afternoon now, I suppose?"

She was her usual happy self. Perhaps, nothing *was* wrong.

"Good afternoon," he replied apprehensively, eyeing her parents. "How are you?" He hated how formal his voice sounded. But at the same time, he was afraid to be his carefree self around Greta's folks.

"I'm good," she said. "Just getting home from church."

Church? he thought. Greta looked like she normally would on any given day. She was wearing tan leggings with a red dress: casual cotton tied at the waist with a white sash. Her hair was haphazardly the same as well, lying about her shoulders, the choppy ends appearing almost sharp. She looked the same as she would on a regular school day. This was Greta, before man, woman and God. "This is my parents," she said. "My dad, Vernon. And my mom, Charlotte."

"It's nice to finally meet you," Vernon said, shaking Blake's hand. The man had a sunny disposition. Tiny spectacles sat upon his elongated nose. He was neatly shaven, and his bald head glistened like a freshly washed car in the afternoon sun; a thin row of brown hair circled his head. He wore a tan suit that was neatly pressed, jacket open. He didn't seem angry. "You live next door? Is that right?"

Blake nodded. "Yes sir. All my life."

"Come on in," Charlotte added. "We always cook a big dinner on Sundays, and there are always leftovers. Maybe if we have a guest, we won't have leftovers and I won't have to put them away." She giggled. Blake had never heard his mother giggle. Charlotte looked so much like her daughter it was scary, like eyeing the future with a rational stare. She was thin and short with long, flowing dark hair. She wore a knee-length dress, white with a flower pattern. "Will you stay for dinner, Blake?"

"Oh, I don't know," Blake said.

"Come on," Vernon said. "You have to. We've heard so much about you from Greta."

Greta blushed.

Vernon went on: "We just have to get to know you. If half of what she tells us is true, you must be an alright kid."

"Please stay for dinner," Greta added.

He couldn't say no to that.

"Sure. I'd love to," he said. "Thank you for the invite, ma'am."

Greta's mother curtsied. "Look at the manners on this boy, Vern. You're very welcome, Blake."

He tried to remember every manner he had ever been taught when talking to Greta's parents. They seemed so different than his own family. Therefore, Blake felt the need to be on his best behavior.

"You kids feel free to go and play," Charlotte said. "Dinner won't be ready for at least a couple of hours or so."

Greta's parents went into the house, leaving Greta and Blake on the porch.

"Have a seat," Greta said, walking over to the swing and sinking into it, crossing her feet as her momentum carried her back and forth.

Blake did as she asked and took a seat beside her.

"Did you get in trouble?" Blake asked.

"Nope, not too bad. They just said that they would rather me tell them where I was going so they wouldn't worry so much. Standard parent stuff. However, here's the story: I told them that we went to see the old house. That part is true. *But*, I also told them we were well on our way home when it started raining and we stayed at your aunt's house until it slacked up a bit. And I definitely didn't tell them anything about Cass. Did you? Tell your folks, I mean."

"Nope. They were asleep when I got home. I climbed up the tree next to my room and went in through the window." Blake sighed. "There's just one problem with your story."

"And what's that?"

"I don't have an aunt that lives up that way," he smiled.

"Oh hush!" Greta said, slapping his shoulder playfully. "It doesn't matter. My parents don't have to know that do they?"

"I see your point," Blake said. "So, anyway, what's for dinner?"

***

Blake and Greta passed the day in the front yard playing basketball on the goal in Greta's driveway, or relaxing in the swing, feeling young and old at the same time. Strangely, this day reminded him of hanging out with Matt; yet at the same time, it was different. He could feel their friendship growing, and loved every minute of it. After all, Greta had said it herself: "Everyone needs friends." And a friend was something Blake hadn't had in quite a while.

But he also admitted, very slowly, as if testing cool waters with the fragile tips of his naked toes, that he felt things for Greta. Things he had never felt before. Feelings that overstepped friendship. Sometimes, he just couldn't help but look at her. There was an air of beauty about her, radiating from the inside out. But he pushed these feelings aside, letting the friendship hold them and take them where it wanted them to go. He trusted their friendship. He had no problem with letting it guide them down unknown paths.

Dinner was delicious. Greta's mother was a terrific cook, not necessarily *better* than his mother, but different. They had beef tips with sautéed vegetables and baked potatoes. Blake sat next to Greta while they ate, and after a while, after getting to know Greta's parents better, he felt more at home than he usually did in his own house, though was careful never to let his manners falter.

Dinner at his house was quite different. Not much was said aside from grace, perhaps the usual chatter about work, chores or Dianne's grades. It was usually much later too. And the potatoes were always fried, never baked.

After dinner, they all walked Blake to the door and warmly oversaw his departure, each expressing their desire for him to return soon.

"Good night," Blake said to all of them. "Thanks for having me. It was great."

Greta hugged him again, squeezing him tightly. Two days in a row! He was quickly getting used to Greta's hugs. When she did, she whispered: "Next week. We'll take Cass's things back to him. That okay with you?"

"Yep," he said.

She could've said, "I'm thinking about shaving your head and using the hair to stuff a pillow. That okay with you?"

He still would have smiled sheepishly and said, "Yep."

But of course, Greta would never say such a thing, as ridiculous or as mean. She would never take advantage of him the way most friends took advantage of each other. Blake believed that with all his heart. That's why his feelings for her were so deep.

He walked home with a smile on his face, having spent a Sunday away from his family. Greta's family was great! The only sadness Blake could muster was wishing his own family were more like hers.

He avoided the last of the mud, which had grown thick as the puddles dried up in the sun, and hopped onto the first step of the house. He looked back towards Greta's house and smiled. The corn swayed slightly in the cool breeze. *The rain likely did it good*, Blake thought. *It'll be a good harvest this year.*

9

Sunday night, Blake decided he would carve Greta something to hang on a necklace. Something simple wouldn't hurt. He went out to the back porch and cut a piece off a sturdy oak branch and set to work. The night air on the porch felt better than the stuffiness of the house and the sounds of the night were more soothing than the buzz of TV and occasional chatter from his family. He sat in a weathered rocking chair and propped his bare feet up on the banisters and cut into the wood unsure what he would make. Luckily, the day had been sunny and the wood had had time to dry out a little.

***

On Monday morning, Blake's English teacher, Mrs. Napier, informed the class that a guest speaker would be visiting them on Thursday, a local author by the name of Alfie Mae Piper. Blake had heard the name before, but had never read any of her books or stories. But still, he found the chance to meet a real writer interesting.

The days that followed passed quickly, the anticipation of lunch and afternoons spent with Greta carried Blake from class to class in instants. They spent evenings playing in the barn, in the cornfield and down the road on Crystal Creek, right up until the sun sank beneath the ridge—alas, until tomorrow.

By the time English class arrived on Thursday Blake had nearly forgotten about the guest. A short lady with graying hair and hunched shoulders sat in the corner next to the blackboard. She wore slacks and a blue buttoned blouse and a pleasant smile dressed her face.

Blake remembered the day's event immediately and knew who she was. He considered saying "hi," but thought better of it. He took his seat with the rest of the class and waited.

"Class, as you remember, we have a very special guest today," Mrs. Napier said. "Please make her feel very welcome, as she was kind enough to come and speak to us today, which as some of you may know is a rare treat. She's one of my favorite authors. She turned our little community into a world of literary merit. Please welcome, Ms. Alfie Mae Piper."

The lady rose to her feet and stood in front of the class with her hands clasped in front of her. Mrs. Napier took a seat in Aflie's chair.

"Good mornin'," she said. Her voice was sweat and quiet, with a slight southern drawl; her eyes reflected the tone of her voice. "Thank you, Mrs. Napier, for that wonderful introduction. Although, I think you may have oversold me." She chuckled.

"Boys and girls, I want to tell you a story about me, about writing, and about this community. I can remember when I was your age. Even then, I wanted to be a writer. I went to a school that consisted of one room. And we never had anyone speak to us about writing professionally, or pursuing any dream that rested outside the mountains. That's why I decided to come here and speak to you today.

"There was one old man who encouraged me when I was little," she said fondly. "And I thank God for him every day of my life. He took an interest in my writing. Back then, I was writing poetry. Really bad poetry I might add," she laughed, as did the class. "A child's poetry. But he showed me the ropes of writing, gave me goals to accomplish, and we'd meet every morning on my way to school and he'd read whatever mess I'd cooked up. That was the highlight of my day."

Blake cradled his chin in the cup of his hand and listened intently to the old woman's words. Todd Hamilton was snickering in the front of the room, but was stifled quickly by Mrs. Napier. Alfie Mae paid him no mind.

"He always called me 'Pip,'" she laughed. "His name was Joseph Bradley. He lived up the road from me, right over here on Caine's Creek, and he'd go for a walk every mornin' right as I was leavin' the house for school. Everybody at school thought he was an odd old man. And I guess he was. But he was such a kind soul. He kept to himself for the most part.

"I tell you this because Mr. Bradley inspired me in more ways than one," she said. "He encouraged me greatly, yes, but I took my first step towards being a serious writer because of his disappearance. It just about floored me when he stopped showing up to walk me to school. I almost stopped writing completely. But I discovered that the only way I could deal with my grief and confusion was to write about it.

"I wrote my first story called 'The Perfect Tree' when I was 20 years old, many years after Mr. Bradley's death. I didn't expect anybody to ever take it seriously or even read it for that matter. I wrote it for me." She paused. "But folks did read it, and some took it seriously. Most regard it as fiction, but not folks around here. I called it 'The Perfect Tree' because that's what Mr. Bradley said he was looking for the last time I ever spoke with him. I can still hear his voice to this day. And sadly, he found it. He found the perfect tree in his own backyard."

Alfie Mae Piper wiped at her eyes with a handkerchief and then stuffed it back into her pants pocket.

"It was Mr. Bradley who gave me the encouragement, the seeds of knowledge that led to the desire for more, and the grief to succeed."

Mrs. Napier squirmed on the edge of her seat.

"Let me ask you this, class," Alfie continued. "How many of you in here have dreams? Dreams that may take you far away from home. A dream that seems impossible."

A few hands shot up around the classroom. Blake found his hand in the air before he knew he had raised it.

"Well, don't let anyone tell you your dreams are out of reach. Fifty-three years ago, an odd old man told me I could do anything. And this odd old lady is here to tell each and every one of you the same thing.

"I won't tell you any more about Mr. Bradley or 'The Perfect Tree.' I encourage you all to read it. You can get it at the local library in a collection of short stories called *Afternoonls: Life as a Series of Type-Os.*"

Blake jotted down Alfie's name and the name of the book in a jagged scribble on the inside of his English textbook on the title page. He listened as Alfie continued throughout the rest of the class, reading some excerpts of her work and offering life advice he didn't quite understand. But still, he teetered on the edge of his seat and soaked up every word, his head propped in his hands, elbows planted upon the wooden desktop.

He needed to make a trip to the library.

***

"She was talking about Mr. Bradley!" Blake said to Greta in between forkfuls of pasty macaroni and cheese. "I have to read that book."

The lunchroom was hot and stuffy—kids packed wall to wall—and smelled of fried chicken and stale milk. The roar of chatter was constant, like a steady chirruping chorus of crickets at dusk.

"That's so cool! I didn't know any authors lived around here. I'll ask my dad if he's heard of her. He reads a lot."

"As soon as I get home I'm begging mom to take me to the library," he said.

"Blake, I don't think I've ever seen you this excited about anything."

"I just never knew there was anything written about that old house or the man who lived there. I thought it was just stuff people made up. I didn't know anything actually happened."

"That is pretty cool. I may give it a read after you're finished."

"Yeah, *if* we can get it from the library to begin with," he said. "There may be a line of other kids from class waiting to get their hands on it as well."

Greta laughed. "I think you overestimate the average kid's desire to read."

***

Blake got off the school bus and took the front steps of his porch in a single leap. He ran to his room and slung his backpack onto his bed, and then ran back downstairs.

"Mom! Mom!" he shouted. "Can you give me a ride to the library?"

She was standing at the sink, suds to her elbows, over a steaming vat of soapy dishes.

"The library?" she said, smiling. "What brought that on?"

He told her about Alfie Mae Piper and her book and how it was about the old house on Caine's Creek.

"You say she grew up here?" she said. "I've never heard of her. But then again, I don't find much time to read. Never did."

"Will you take me?" Blake pleaded.

"Blake, I can't this evening. I have to get these dishes done and get supper on the table. Maybe tomorrow." She chuckled, "library," and went back to her work.

Outside, the day had grown humid beneath a cloudless sky. Blake rambled about the sandy driveway, eyes on the ground watching the swirls of dust his dragging feet kicked up.

"Blake!" Greta yelled from down the road, running towards him. "Your mom taking you to the library?"

"Nope," he shouted back.

"Well, mine will! Ask your mom if you can go!"

She was still yelling even though she was now standing next to him panting from the brisk run.

"What is all this yelling about?" Patty asked from the porch, craning her head out the screen door.

"Greta's mom is taking her to the library," Blake said. "Can I go?"

"So, this is the Greta from next door?"

"Yes, ma'am," Greta said. "Nice to meet you."

"Likewise," Patty nodded. "You can go, Blake. Just try not to be out too late."

"Sure thing!"

Blake and Greta ran side by side back to Greta's house, where Charlotte was waiting in the driver's seat of the black sedan with the motor running. Blake climbed into the backseat, Greta into the front.

"Thanks for taking us," Blake said. "I really appreciate it."

"It's no problem," Charlotte said, eyeing him over top of her sunglasses through the rearview mirror. "I was shocked to hear you kids desperately want to read. I'm happy to be of service."

The library was only a 20-minute drive down a series of modest two-lane roads. Blake couldn't recall ever going to this library. He'd used the one at school and had been to the book fair every year. He expected the parking lot to be full and the place to be swarming with folks ransacking disheveled racks of free books. Instead, the parking lot held only four occupied spaces, 2 cars, a truck and a van. The rest of the lot was vacant.

Charlotte parked the car and the three of them walked to the front of the building. Blake pushed open the heavy door and held it for Greta and her mother. The air was thick with the smell of dusty, aging paper and mildewing carpet. A meek woman with short, black hair sat behind a grand desk made of varnished oak, her fingers busy upon a keyboard as her eyes peered over thin-rimmed glasses.

Greta was right about one thing: the place seemed deserted aside from the lady at the counter and very few others. Two people were using large, gray, IBM computers quietly, with giant, spongy headphones pulled over their ears, while another large man in overalls browsed the VHS tapes available for check out. Shelves of books lined the walls and stood in rows all the way to the back of the building. There were so many Blake didn't know where to begin searching for Alfie Mae Piper's book.

He approached the woman at the counter as Greta and her mother tip-toed to the tall stacks of fiction.

"Excuse me, ma'am," he said.

She looked up from her task and smiled warmly. "Yes, can I help you?" Her name tag read "Bobbi."

"I'm looking for a book."

"I think I can help you," she smiled. "We have plenty of books. Which one in particular are you looking for?"

"*Afternoonls?* By Alfie Mae Piper."

"Aah, yes. Terrific collection of short stories," she said. "Many about our little hometown of Hemingford."

"Is it in?" Blake asked.

"I believe so," Bobbi said. "Right this way. In our local authors section."

Blake followed her to the shelves lining the left side of the wall. The shelves were much shorter here, as they dipped in height to allow for windows. The librarian squatted down and ran a slender finger along the worn spines of dusty books.

"Here it is," she said, taking out an average-sized book of about 250 yellowing pages. The cover was a light mauve with a black spine. She handed Blake the book, smiled warmly and walked back towards the desk, her footfalls making literally no noise.

Blake flipped it open with eager hands and fumbled to the table of contents.

"*The Perfect Tree*. Page 211."

He cascaded the pages starting from the back until he found page 211. He sat down in the floor with his back to the shelf and began to read. By the time he finished the last line of the 23-page short story, Greta stood before him with a stack of books cradled in her arms. Blake could see the spines and recognized them all: *Lord of the Flies*, by William Golding, *The Wizard of Oz*, by Frank L. Baum, *The Hobbit*, by J.R. R. Tolkien, and *Where the Red Fern Grows*, by Wilson Rawls.

"Mom says I need to read these, and I guess they look interesting enough. Even though I've seen the Wizard of Oz movie, she tells me the book's different." She looked up from the stack. "Are you crying?"

A single tear budded at the corner of Blake's left eye, and he could feel it sting before it rolled down his cheek. He nodded, but smiled.

"That must be one hell of a book," Greta said.

10

After obtaining library cards, Blake checked out *Afternoonls* and Greta a stack of her mother's recommendations. Blake read well into the morning hours, and by 3:30 he had finished every story in the book, and had, in fact, read *The Perfect Tree* twice. The story made him long to see the old house again.

The week passed quickly. Before Blake and Greta knew it, Friday was over as quick as Monday had begun and they were once again riding the jostling school bus home to another weekend—trees, creeks and bottoms all rushing by and blending together in the windows.

"Same time tomorrow?" Greta said, leaning up over one of the weathered green seats.

"Yep, sounds good to me," Blake answered. "I'm really looking forward to seeing the old house again."

"That's a welcome change of spirit," Greta laughed. "I thought I was going to have to tie you up and drag you to get you to go last weekend."

"I just figure that seeing it after reading that book will be different, I guess."

"That's the spirit!" Greta cried, mockingly punching Blake in the jaw. "It'll seem more real knowing that all those stories you hear about the house are true. I figured that would make the place seem creepier."

"Exactly!" Blake said. "It makes it seem *real*. Not like that old place is crawling with ghosts or anything, but like something bad really happened there. It makes it seem more like history than legend. Does that make sense?"

"Perfect sense," she said. "Maybe we should ride bikes this time. We'd probably save a lot of time."

"That may be the best idea you've ever had, Gretchen Wills."

"Easy on the 'Gretchen,'" she said in a serious tone, but stared at him with playful blue eyes.

They departed the bus and went their separate ways, right where the mailboxes stood side by side, 1531 and 1541 Crystal Creek Road. Blake wasn't sure, but he thought he noticed Van glaring at them from a seat in the back of the bus as they were making their way towards the front to exit. Blake found it strange that Van hadn't said anything to them since their exchange on the bus last week. He had been pleasantly distant.

"I'll see you in the morning," Greta called, waving her arms vigorously from half way down her driveway.

"Bright and early," Blake replied, offering a similar gesture. As far as he was concerned, morning couldn't come early enough.

***

Blake finished carving the necklace and sanded it as smooth as its small frame would allow. It was an owl with wings folded at its sides and great big eyes with nearly impossible detail, Blake having added a fine coat of Dianne's yellow fingernail polish for accents. He attached a tiny silver hoop at the top of its head and strung an old silver chain through, then coated it in clear-coat varnish and set it in front of the noisy box fan in his room to dry.

He slept well, as well as one could beneath such anticipation as the next day held. And it wasn't just Greta. He found that he was actually thinking a lot about Mr. Bradley, Alfie Mae Piper, Cass, and what he was doing up in that old house. He fathomed stories in his mind that led the weathered man through various points of adventure, all of which ended with him beneath the sagging roof of the old house at the head of Caine's Creek.

But surely, the man was so rotten, so mean, that he didn't deserve such thoughts. He had a story. Everybody does. But he wasn't about to tell it, and Blake wasn't about to ask.

Blake had done all of his chores immediately after school, working well into the evening, so that his Saturday would be free. He had washed the old Chevy and marveled at its gleam after a fresh wash, despite its years; he had moved all the stout rocking chairs from the porch and scrubbed it, stooped over a bucket with a soapy sponge in hand; he had fed and watered Aphrodite and tidied up the barn thinking the whole time that no matter how tidy a barn gets, it's still going to reminisce of cow shit. After finishing the carving, he went to bed with tired bones, joints that seemed coated with chalk, and feet that felt like they made a life's journey with nothing to show at the end but torn calluses

The next morning when Blake descended the stairs, dressed in blue jean shorts with Greta's necklace in the pocket and a gray pocket T-shirt, backpack slung over one shoulder ready to fill with food for the road, he was greeted with the sound of voices and clatter instead of silence. His family stared at him blankly.

"What are you guys doing up so early?" Blake said.

"I got a phone call," Elden said, sipping a cup of steaming coffee. "Early. Too early for it to be any kind of good news."

Blake's eyes settled on his father. His forehead bore deep-set lines of worry and his face was taught, lips pursed.

"Blake come and have some breakfast," Patty said. She hurried back to the stove to a simmering pan that Blake hadn't noticed until now. From the smell that filled the room, bacon. She looked twice as concerned as his father. Blake was curious. He had never seen his parents this upset.

Though he didn't necessarily want to, Blake took a seat at the table across from Dianne. Her eyes were on her cup of milk and she didn't look up to greet him.

"So, what's wrong?" Blake said.

His parents exchanged looks before his father spoke. Dianne's lips begin to quiver just before she released a helpless sob.

"Two people were killed on Harker's Branch," Elden said. "They found the bodies last night. But they think they've been dead for a couple of weeks."

It took Blake a moment to realize the horror of what his father just said. He had never known anyone to die, though at times, it felt that Matt had died since he had moved away. Harker's Branch was only a few miles from Crystal Creek—just two miles down the two-lane road then turn left—and to have someone murdered that close to home meant two things: the first, that the family was in danger simply based on relativity; the second, it was more than likely someone they knew.

"Who was it?" Blake asked, not realizing he had said anything until the words were already out.

His father locked his eyes on Blake's. Sternness seemed a priority.

"Arthur and Dory," he said. "Jenna may be coming home from college to stay with us for a little while. At least until after the funeral."

Blake's fingers went numb, right up to the tips. His throat became dry, and when he opened his mouth to speak nothing came out but a dry rasp. He hadn't expected something so terrible to happen to members of his own family. *Things like this always happened to other people,* he thought. *In the news or in movies and books. Never to anyone you know, never to your own family.*

Blake actually despised his uncle, but he had always been close to Jenna, though she was quite older than him. Before she left for college the previous year, Blake would visit often, even spend the night occasionally. She was the only cousin he ever spent time with. They would play outside most of the time, or draw in her room, and spend as much time away from Arthur as possible, who stank of whiskey and cigars, and never had a kind word to offer. Dory always kept the house spotless, but she could never quite stamp out the stench of Arthur. The whole family always gathered at Arthur and Dory's for Thanksgiving dinner, and sometimes for Christmas. Even in the glory of a family gathering, Arthur made most people uncomfortable. It bothered Blake that his aunt would never make eye contact with Arthur, even when speaking directly to him or delivering him a beverage as he sat matted to his favorite arm chair in the living room.

"I—I—" He struggled to regain tonality. "I haven't seen Jenna since Christmas." He felt silly at the words coming out of his mouth. But he felt he needed to talk.

"Listen, Blake," Patty said. "We want you to stay close to the house for the next week or so, okay?"

"I can't," Blake said. "I have somewhere to be."

"Blake, you are 12 years old! Where do you need to be? What is so important?" His mother's voice rose. Tears began to leak from her eyes.

"I'll be alright," Blake said, remaining calm, or at the very least, docile. He stood up. "I have to go now."

"Blake, I'm at the end of my rope," she screamed. "Now sit down!"

"I'm just going out in the yard, Mom," he said, and patted her arm. "I just need some time to think."

She sat down, defeated, and continued to cry. Blake hugged her shoulders and kissed her temple before leaving the room. His mother didn't bother to stop him.

"Blake," his father said in a resonating deep voice, demanding. "Don't go too far."

***

Blake wondered around outside the house for a little while, his eyes fixed on the ground beneath his feet, unaware of his surroundings. He had forgotten all about Greta and the day ahead until he heard her voice call to him.

"Blake! Where have you been? Did you oversleep?"

She came rushing towards him with her backpack strapped over her shoulders, and pushing a clattering blue bicycle. The smile on her face seemed so otherworldly to him. He felt like his face would never look like that again. But he didn't hate her for it the way some people would, reacting in such a childish manner. He admired her for her character, could never loathe it no matter how it contrasted with his own.

He looked at her with pleading eyes and noticed he still had his backpack over his shoulder. He took it off and dropped it to the grass. Greta's smile faded slowly. She dropped her bike and sat down beside him, placing an arm around his shoulder.

"What's wrong?"

Blake wanted to answer immediately, but his voice swelled with sorrow until it burst in a shower of tears. He buried his face in Greta's shoulder and sobbed, totally absent. She held his head and stroked his hair while he cried.

When the tears had eased, Blake rose up to look at Greta, but first saw the dark red splotches of tears he had left on her pink shirt. It looked like a face etched into the material, crying or melting.

"Sorry about your shirt," he said.

"Don't be stupid, Blake. You know I don't care about the shirt. Cry all you want. But please, tell me what's wrong."

Blake looked over his shoulder at the house.

"I'll be right back," he said.

He ran to the house, up the steps, and stuck his head inside the front door.

"Mom! Dad! I'm going to play with Greta for a little while," he shouted.

"Stay close to the house," Elden said. He came out of the kitchen and stood close enough for Blake to touch. Blake had no idea he was so close.

"I know, Dad," Blake said, pleading. He lowered his voice to almost a whisper. "I just need to get out of here for a little while. I need to get my mind off everything. I'll stay close by."

Clearly, Blake had been crying. His streaked red face and his cracking voice betrayed his thin-lipped attempt at smiling.

He had never approached his father with such a permissive tone. He had always talked to him as though one man was addressing another man. This conversation felt foreign to him, like it was buried deep in a dream. If only it were a dream—no more dead relatives, no more pleading with his father. He felt so numb, yet his chest felt as though it were about to burst.

"Okay," Elden said. "Just stay close. We just worry about you, son."

He nodded to his father, attempting to return their usual adult dynamic, as though trying to regain some of the dignity he had just offered away.

He turned and ran back to the corn field where Greta sat waiting for him next to her toppled bicycle.

"Blake, what's going on?" she said.

"Let's go. I'll tell you on the way."

Blake's bicycle was leaning beside the barn. He couldn't remember riding it since before Matt left. He retrieved it and the two children peddled their way to the end of the driveway, and then further down Crystal Creek. Blake stood on the pedals and let the bicycle glide and the wind pelted his face with cool air. He almost felt like nothing was wrong, but he couldn't push the truth from his mind. He felt like he had suddenly found himself inside a story he was reading, turning page after page with anticipation, looking on to whatever end, whether it be bitter or redeeming.

"Hold up," Greta shouted, pulling her bike up beside his as they sped down the gritty roadway. "Pull it over!"

As much as he just wanted to keep going, Blake reluctantly stepped back on his footbrake and brought the bicycle to a solid stop, skidding through dirt, kicking up a cloud of dust and leaving a healthy tire track in the process.

"What is wrong?" Greta demanded. "Until the other day, I couldn't even *picture* you crying."

Blake looked at Greta sternly, until he felt that he looked something like his father attempting to hold a gaze. He then dropped his stare to the road and searched there for answers, for a way to tell Greta his problems. He opened his mouth, and let the words pour out.

"My aunt and uncle were murdered," he said.

Greta's mouth gaped. Suddenly all the sounds typically paid little mind invaded the otherwise silent world: a trickling creek parallel to the road; a rusty spring in a bicycle seat, shifting beneath nervous weight; taciturn heaving, an internal attempt for exchange, an effort for oxygen.

"Are you playing with me?" Greta finally said, breaking the awful stillness. "You're joking." She smiled, but the corners of her mouth twitched slightly.

"It's no joke," Blake said. "I wish it was."

He relayed the story to Greta, told her everything that had happened that morning, including that his parents didn't want him to go very far away from the farm. He also told her everything his father had told him about the murders.

"Murder?" Greta said. "Way out in the sticks? I've heard stuff like this in the news when I lived in Greenwich, but I never expected it here."

"Goes to show that evil is everywhere. I guess nobody is really ever safe."

Blake almost laughed at how morbid he sounded. But when he didn't, it only made his words seem more chilling.

"I take it your parents don't know?" Blake asked.

"I suppose not," Greta said. "If they do, they haven't mentioned it to me."

"Hmm."

"We can just hang out around your place," Greta said. "Cass can come and get his own things."

"No," Blake said. "I want to go, now more than ever. I need to get away from the house. I think my mom is on the verge of a nervous breakdown."

He fumbled in his pocket absently and felt the tiny wooden carving and pulled it out. The owl swayed at the end of the old silver chain.

"What's that?"

"Something I made for you," he said.

"Blake you don't need to make me anything." Her eyes drooped to sadness but the corners of her mouth turned up in sympathy.

"Turn around," he said. "I want you to have it."

Greta turned around and sighed, lifting her hair away from her neck so he could fasten the small silver clasp.

"There," he said. She turned around and he admired his work, dangling just below the dip between her clavicles. The clear-coat had turned the bird a darker shade of brown in places but all its fine detail still glimmered in the daylight.

"Thank you," she said meekly.

"You're welcome," he said. "Let's go."

"But won't you get in trouble?" Greta said. "I mean serious trouble, Blake. And your mom probably needs you."

"I ain't worried about trouble right now. I just need to get away from all this. And Mom has Dad and Dianne. She don't need me. Now, let's get going. We have a long trip ahead."

II

The trip was much shorter on bicycles, but also more taxing when the narrow roads shifted to even a slight incline. Still, even considering the late start, they were at the mouth of Caine's Creek just before noon. And though it was difficult to talk while speeding along on bikes, the trip was still enjoyable. They made figure 8s in the road, and raced on straight stretches, Blake trying desperately to ignore the horrors he had left at home.

After an hour's ride out of Crystal Creek and along the main two-lane road, they dismounted their bicycles just a little ways into Caine's Creek. They ran urgent hands through disheveled, wind-blown hair.

"One thing about this road," Blake said. "It's slightly uphill the rest of the way, so if you want to get off and walk for a little while, that's fine with me. I'm beat."

"Yeah. Riding the whole way up this road would be a nightmare for my calves. We're making good time, though. Let's walk for a while."

She leaned her bike against a tree and dug in her backpack until she withdrew her father's canteen. She took a long drink and wiped the excess water from her lips before handing the container to Blake. He drank, feeling each gulp cool his body. Despite the distance they had made in the sweltering sun, the water was surprisingly cool. The canteen was indeed doing its job.

"Whew," Greta said, after taking another drink. "This thing is a lifesaver, huh?" She handed the canteen back to Blake for one more drink before putting it back in her pack.

"Definitely," Blake said.

They began pushing their bikes up the roadway, occasionally seeing a Caine's Creek resident out and about in their yard, weeding flower beds or mowing grass with a painfully loud gas-powered mower. Blake wondered if any of them knew of Alfie or Joseph Bradley. But then a terrible realization invaded his mind and his sweat instantly turned cold: Van Dougherty lived somewhere up this way. Blake was nearly sure of it. He decided not to say anything. After all, they hadn't ran into him on their last trip, and this time they had the option to speed away on bicycles should the need arise.

They walked into deep shade. The trees above them had entwined, lacing branch tips longingly together like two lovers being separated by an unforeseen force; in this case, the force being a tiny one-lane roadway built by man and misunderstood by nature.

"Just imagine how easy it will be to ride out of here," Blake said. "What goes up has to come down. It'll be all downhill. Imagine how fast we can go!"

"Yeah," Greta said, sounding relieved. "We definitely shouldn't have a problem getting home before dark this time."

"I'm not worried about it," Blake said. "We'll get home when we get home."

Greta sighed. "I'd really like to be home before dark, though," she said. "It's sort of scary, with what happened and all. I sort of understand where your mom's coming from, wanting to keep you close to home." Her face turned red and she hung her head.

Blake looked at her suddenly, eyes wide. For a moment he didn't speak, but then he smiled.

"I guess you're right," he said. "Home before dark it is."

***

They continued walking for the next hour or so without stopping. Caine's Creek could definitely be considered a creepy place, filled with deep shadows in the daytime, soggy ground coated with mud and moss; the bank opposite the tiny creek was laden with thick underbrush gathered tight around the base of trees that stretched high above them. By the time they were at the halfway point, the trees overhead were so dense the day had nearly became dusk, despite a vibrant sun shining above.

"Right up there is the lake I was telling you about," Blake said, pointing to a tiny dirt path, barely big enough to walk on, with sides crowded by brush and briars that led off the one-lane main road of Caine's Creek.

"You mean the lake where the old man's daughter drowned?"

"Yep, that's the one. His name was Joseph Bradley." It no longer seemed appropriate to call him "the old man."

Blake thought of Mr. Bradley losing his family, and then his mind; he then thought of his recently lost family members. He began to understand overwhelming sadness. He imagined that he had lost his parents or Greta. Then he thought of how Jenna must feel. She *did* lose her parents. It was all too much to think about.

The sun was still shining above the trees overhead when they reached the house, a definite improvement since the last time. Yet the house didn't look much different in the sun than it did at dusk. Sparse, glimmering splotches of light navigated the branches overhead and lit upon the house like fireflies. It seemed sad from neglect, its walls scarred and windows filthy. The yard was still an overgrown mass of weeds. Shadows fell beneath the windows like bags beneath the eyes. A house that hadn't slept, but instead set to draw dampness and mildew, rotting silently, left to itself.

Blake eyed the house apprehensively, Aflie Mae's words still vibrant in his mind; but Greta pushed aside the rotting gate without any caution whatsoever. The gate, barely hanging on by one last rusted hinge, scraped the dirt with the bottoms of its worm-eaten planks. Greta entered the yard as though visiting a friend's house.

She was already on the porch by the time Blake had entered the yard, and out of good-mannered habit, shut the gate behind him.

"Greta!" he whispered. "Wait. Maybe we could just leave his stuff by the gate, or on the porch. What do you think?" This time it wasn't fear that repelled Blake from the house. It was sadness. It was all too vivid now. He could almost see Mr. Bradley with his gnarled, old walking stick easing carefully down the stone steps at the entrance to the yard, or sitting on the porch sipping coffee, or walking out back to take in the shade one last time, caressing the tire swing where his daughter likely played when she were alive, finally driving himself to no longer bear the burdens of this earth.

"Oh come on," Greta said with disappointment, hands on her hips. "We came all this way. I want to see Cass. Do you think he would have let us borrow his stuff in the first place if he didn't want us to come back?"

Blake paused a moment, contemplating. His limbs felt tingly and absent.

"But he said ... " Blake considered the possibility that Greta was right. "But he said he didn't want us to come back. That he wouldn't tell if we didn't tell and that we should just stay away."

"You bought that?" Greta said. "That's just a tough-guy act. I think he likes us. He likes us at least enough not to let us walk home in the rain without a flashlight and raincoat."

Before Blake could say another word of discouragement, Greta turned and knocked loudly on the wobbly screen door. Her knuckles sent flecks of dried paint fluttering down to the weathered wood of the porch.

"Greta, I'm not sure I trust him," Blake said, thinking of what had happened to his aunt and uncle. After all, Cass was a stranger, not just to them, but to Hemingford. But then again, were he rank with murderous intent, he had every chance to hurt the two of them during their last visit.

Greta waited for a brief moment, and then knocked again.

The door cracked open slightly.

"Why don't you kids meet me out back?" Cass said, with only a sliver of his face visible between the door and the enjambment. "D'you bring my stuff?"

"Yep, we sure did," Greta said, smiling. "That was very nice of you to let us borrow it like that. Thanks. Thanks a lot."

"Psshhh," Cass hissed. "I didn't do it to be nice. I just didn't see the point in having two kids wanderin' around all night in the rain, catching their death of cold. Ain't nobody ever gonna say that I killed two little kids 'cause I was stingy with my rain coat."

Blake's ears perked at the word kill and his body shivered.

"Well, I still think it was nice," Greta said. But before she was halfway through her sentence, Cass closed the door with a loud thud.

"He doesn't seem too happy to see us if you ask me," Blake said. "Let's just leave the stuff on the porch and get the hell out of here!"

"He asked us to come out back," Greta said.

"Maybe he wants us out there so nobody will see him kidnap us ... or worse!" Blake said through gritted teeth.

"Blake Kiser! You ought to be ashamed! Why would you think something like that? Besides if he—"

"I know," Blake said. "If he was going to hurt us, he had the perfect chance. I know."

"He probably just doesn't want anybody to know that he's living here," Greta said.

"And you don't think that's a little shady?"

Greta rolled her eyes.

She hurried off the porch and around the side of the house before Blake could get another word in. Blake followed. It once again shocked him how soggy the ground was along the side of the old house. The soil was damp and there was moss growing along the ground beneath the struggling grass that was sure to die, much unlike the thick weeds that crowded the front lawn. Trees overhung the area completely, touching the roof of the house, creating a canopy that would not grant the sun admittance.

Cass was sitting on the back stoop where they had last seen him the previous weekend. He had a pocket knife in his hand, contently whittling away at a gnarled piece of wood.

"Where's my stuff?" he said without looking up.

"Right here," Greta said, shedding her backpack which held Cass's things. She set the backpack on the ground and unzipped it.

"Bring 'em over here," Cass said.

Blake reached and grabbed the flashlight and raincoat before Greta had the chance. He approached Cass cautiously. Such a harsh personality always created reproach in Blake's mind. He stood before Cass with the borrowed items in hand.

Cass said, "Just set 'em down and you all be on your way."

Blake placed the items on the ground, and in doing so, noticed that Cass was not absently carving the small piece of wood, but rather, was whittling it into a tiny statue, a rendition of a miniature wolf.

"That's pretty good," Blake said watchfully before he caught himself.

Cass looked up for the first time since they had entered the backyard.

"Is it now?" Cass said. "Who made you the judge?"

"Nobody," Blake said, voice slightly trembling. "I've just done my share of whittling, I suppose."

"Oh? You whittle, do ya? You any good?" Cass asked with a grin that boasted of entertaining a silly notion.

"I can show you," Blake said, becoming somewhat defensive at Cass's patronization. "Greta! Come here for a second."

Greta, who had been somewhat forgotten by Blake and Cass, was gleefully making wide circles in the rotating tire swing. She called out shrill cries of excitement as the rope began to twist and spin her around.

"Greta!" Blake repeated, somewhat amused. "I want to show Cass your necklace."

She looked up, acknowledging Blake's request.

"One more round, Blake!" she cried.

She placed the tire horizontally around her waist and stepped back until the rope would not permit her to go any further. But instead of swinging forward, as one would do on a normal swing, she swung out to the side, causing the tire-swing to once again create wide circles while Greta laid back, her head dangling towards the ground, her feet in the air.

In the midst of this wide swing the rope holding the tire snapped and Greta smacked the ground with a solid thud. Her cries of joy ceased when she hit to the ground. Blake immediately sprinted across the backyard and to her side. To her credit, and to Blake's astonishment, she did not cry.

"I'm fine," she said, rubbing her hip and the small of her back as she crawled out of the tire. "Nothing broke but my ego. It figures that thing would break. How old do you think it is?"

"Yeah. I'm not sure. You sure you're okay?" Blake said.

"I'm good," she said, getting to her feet still holding her back. "Takes more than that to keep me down."

"You okay, little girl?" Cass said. "What was your name again?"

"Greta," she said. "And yes. I'm fine."

"And you are?" Cass said, looking peripherally at Blake.

"That's Blake," Greta said, raking at the scuffs of grass stain on the seat of her shorts.

"And Blake knows how to whittle, does he?"

Cass leaned down and eyed the tiny wooden bird that hung from Greta's neck. He examined it thoroughly with his eyes, but never touched it.

"That's a good amount of detail," he said, looking at Blake. "Not bad for a kid."

"For a kid?" Blake said, his temper beginning to spark. "I think that one turned out really good. I worked hard on it! I'd like to see you carve a better one!"

Cass chuckled. "Easy boy," he said. "I didn't mean no offense. I just meant that if you're this good now, I'd like to see what you can do when you grow up."

Blake began to speak, but stopped, shocked at Cass's words. He had expected a retort, not a compliment.

"You all wanna see something?" Cass said.

Blake and Greta exchanged glances.

"Follow me."

93

They followed him to the back stoop where he had been whittling when they arrived, but to their surprise, he opened the back door of the house and walked inside, beckoning for them to follow with a motion of his hand. Blake followed him inside, his curiosity finally getting the better of him, Greta at his heels.

The inside of the house was dark, the only light spilling in through parted curtains, the windows covered with grime. Some of the furniture was under plastic, though a few pieces had been uncovered and recently used. The shelves were lined with dusty old books, and in one corner of the room stood a stack of boxes. One of the top boxes stood open, a stack of disorderly papers visible beneath the opened, crinkled flaps.

"Where did all this stuff come from, Mr. Blighly?" Greta asked. "Was it here when you moved in?"

Cass looked at her dauntingly, but quickly averted his glare, covering his tracks with a smile.

"Well, first of all, Greta. You call me Cass. No more Mr. Blighly. That okay with you?"

Greta nodded. Blake was barely paying attention to their conversation, but instead taking in the eerie chill, born of the years he had spent regarding this house as "haunted" and made worse by the lingering details of *The Perfect Tree*. Never had Blake dreamed he would set foot inside this place. He expected something horrid, perhaps the phantom of the old man, neck broken and swaying to the side, ambulating about from place to place, gathering intangible memoirs from its old life.

"To answer your question, Greta, all this junk *was* here when I moved in. They told me it came with the house, was mine, and to do what I want with it. I just figure I'd use it, since I ain't got no stuff of my own."

"That makes sense," Greta said. "But don't you think you could have cleaned it up a little."

"I'll live the way I want to!" Cass bellowed. "You understand?"

Greta shrank. Cass's voice echoed off the 10-foot ceilings in resonating low tones.

"So you *have* decided to buy the place?" Greta said.

"I think I will," Cass said. "It's back out of the way so I won't be bothered all the time. Good and shady too."

"I'm glad to hear it," Greta said. "I think you'll like it here. I just moved here a little while ago and I love it so far. If you ever need any help..."

She stopped speaking when she noticed Cass had turned and walked towards the other side of the room.

"Boy, get over here," Cass said. "I especially want you to see this."

Blake heard Cass call to him, but was centered on his surroundings, a constant chill lingering along the base of his neck causing the tiny hairs there to stand.

"Hey!" Cass said again, louder.

Blake jerked out of his fixation. "What?"

"I want to show you this," Cass said. "Now come on. Follow me."

Cass walked through a doorway, lacking a door, and into a room that seemed too dark to see anything inside. Greta took Blake's hand and they followed him. Despite the circumstances, Blake grinned. Greta's hand was cold and she held on tightly.

Once inside, Cass walked to the far side of the dim room and tossed back two dark curtains. Sunlight poured in, mingling with the stir of dust that flew from the disturbed curtains. Cass motioned them closer with a wave of his hand. When Blake and Greta arrived next to him, he pointed at a table with several wooden figurines on it, some large, some small, all hand carved from pieces of maple and oak. Some still bore the scent of fresh cut tree limbs.

"Did you carve these?" Blake asked.

Cass nodded.

Blake picked up one of the tiny figures. It was a tree, the trunk of which was no bigger than Blake's pinky-finger; the barren boughs snaked off into several directions, creating a cluster of branches that sprung from the trunk in sporadic motions.

"Wow," Blake said under his breath. "How did you get so good at this?"

"Well, let's just say I have a lot of spare time. So, you see what I mean, kid? You're good." Cass smirked sardonically. "But you've still got a ways to go."

Blake regarded him with scornful derision. He tossed the tiny tree back on the table. It toppled over, falling into several other nearby statuettes.

"Hey! Careful with those, boy!" Cass shouted, and slammed his hand down onto the table where the carvings stood, the force of which toppled even more over.

"Sorry," Blake said, torn between fear and distaste. It wasn't that he regarded himself as a great carver, but he felt as though Cass's comments were downplaying his efforts towards his gift for Greta. He had been so proud of the work he had put into the little owl, taking the time to create fine notches, so that the wings resembled feathers instead of scathed bare wood.

"Blake, we should probably be heading home, don't you think?" Greta said, tugging at his arm.

"Yeah, I guess we should."

"Yeah, that's right. You all get out of here," Cass said. "And let me be."

Blake felt Greta's grip on his arm tighten. He understood how she felt. He was scared too. But once they were outside, he would comfort her, maybe even hug her and pat her head as it lay on his shoulder.

But to his surprise, Greta released his arm after a final squeeze. She had turned to Cass and scowled intensely. Blake had never seen such a look on Greta's face, not even during her encounter with Van. Normally, she was the optimistic voice of reason—his escape from his own mourning, his temper, his morose pessimism.

"Who do you think you are?" Greta shouted, her voice loud throughout the silent house, though not quite resonating as Cass's had. "Why do you think you can talk to us like that?"

Cass began to speak, but Greta persisted.

"One minute you're being nice and inviting us into your home, showing us your art, and the next minute you're telling us what a nuisance we are and telling us to leave. You're a real jackass, you know that? You have serious issues!"

Greta turned and took hold of Blake's hand again and marched defiantly towards the door.

"Little girl!" Cass shouted. "Er, umm, Greta! You'd better hold your tongue before you—"

Cass's voice trailed off and vanished when they closed the backdoor behind them, leaving them to the subtle sounds of twilight that occupied the chilly backyard.

Blake looked at Greta with an open jaw, shocked. Her hand, nestled into his, began to tremble. Greta let go of his hand and covered her face. She sank down onto the stoop and began to cry. Blake was shaking too, afraid that Cass would burst through the back door at any moment to unleash his uncontrolled wrath on both of them, turning Greta's nerve into a regrettable lesson.

But he gathered his courage and sat down beside her.

"Hey. It's okay," he said. He cautiously placed his hand on her shoulder.

Greta turned and buried her face into Blake's chest and sobbed. "How can he be so mean? How can he treat us like that?" She let out an echoing scream, somewhere between a cry and a growl. "It pisses me off!"

The stream of rhetorical conversation came from Greta's lips in a constant, barely comprehensible flow. Blake didn't bother answering her questions, but simply allowed her to cry as he held her and stared off into the gathering night. Once the sobs began to disperse, he lifted her chin to look at her. Her face was streaked with tears, and a trickle of snot had gathered along her top lip.

"You were so brave," Blake said. "And I've never seen you look so pretty."

Greta's lips turned up slightly and she giggled in between sobs.

"Pretty? No one has ever told me that before," she said. "I've heard 'weird, scrawny, odd,' and even 'ugly.' But never 'pretty.'"

Blake allowed himself to laugh slightly. She hugged him so tight he held his breath.

"You're the best friend I've ever had," Greta said.

"Same here," Blake replied, feeling a part of Matt's memory fade. But it was true. "You're the best friend I could ever want."

12

By the time Blake and Greta started home, it was dark, so dark that riding a bicycle would be dangerous on Caine's Creek. They pushed their bikes along, and walked briskly so they wouldn't be too late getting home. Once they were out of Caine's Creek, Blake thought the moon would provide enough light so that they could ride and not worry about the dangers of darkness.

The canopy of trees overhead hid the sky from them, keeping the clouds, the stars, even the moon a secret. The occasional night sounds broke the silence as well as the monotonous shuffling of their feet against the road.

Something called into the night, a shrill noise, sharp among the other damp night sounds of frogs, crickets, and trickling water. Greta gasped, jumped, and peered around searching for the source of the sound. Blake couldn't help but chuckle.

"Relax," Blake said, attempting to quell his laughter. "It's just a screech owl. It won't hurt you."

"A what?"

"Oh yeah, I forgot. City girl," Blake said, playfully.

"Hey, watch that 'city girl' stuff, kid-o," Greta said, fighting off a smile. "What was that?" She persisted.

"It's a screech owl," Blake said. "It's not mad or anything. That's just what they sound like. Looks kind of like this," he said, giving the owl at her neck a gentle tug.

"Why have I never heard it before?" Greta said defiantly.

"They only come out late at night."

"Oh, so they're nocturnal?" Greta said.

"Noc-what?"

Greta laughed, covering her mouth with her hand to suppress the laughter.

"Shhh!" Blake said.

"What's the matter, country boy? Can't take a retort?" she giggled.

"No, shhh!" Blake persisted. "I thought I saw something up there."

"Up where?" Greta said, no longer laughing, but peering into the darkness ahead.

"Up ahead. I thought I saw something move in the road."

It was so dark Blake could barely make out the concerned look on Greta's face. He squinted and peered ahead, but it didn't help much. They had stopped moving at this point, and were standing perfectly still in the middle of the tiny one-lane road.

Blake stepped forward in an act of subconscious intrepidity. The darkness remained thick, but slowly subsided as their eyes adjusted, ever so slightly, to reveal the previously cloaked terrain. Still, he saw nothing.

"I guess it was my imagination," Blake said.

No sooner than the words were out of his mouth, Blake felt a strong thud against the side of his head. He fell to the ground, his elbows scraping to a halt against the harsh roadway. He heard Greta scream from where he lay.

She was backing away, trembling hands covering her fearful yells.

Blake started to get to his feet, but was kicked hard in the ribs. He fell to his side, and lay coughing in the darkness.

Greta rushed to his side, screaming at the figures that accompanied them in the night. She threw a punch and Blake heard it connect with a sturdy smack. She then kicked, but didn't hit anything at all. Someone hit Greta in the temple. She reeled and fell to the ground. She tried to get up, but kept stumbling as three sets of worn work boots circled her.

"Isn't it a little late for you kids to be out by yourselves?" a familiar voice called. "I mean, what if somebody like us came along?"

"That little bitch hit me!" another voiced said angrily.

"Calm down, Ronnie," the first voice said.

"Hey, don't hold me back," Ronnie said. "Nobody hits me and gets away with it!"

"Haha! Ronnie got beat up by a girl!" A third voice. A girl's voice.

"Hey, come on guys! Cool it!" the familiar voice said. "The question is, 'what are we gonna do with these kids?' They really shouldn't be out so late, eh? We should teach them a lesson." He sneered. "It may save their lives one day."

Blake placed the voice. It was Van. He would know it anywhere.

"That sounds good," Ronnie said. "Me first! Me and the girl!"

Greta whimpered as she uselessly tried once more to push herself up. Blake was almost to his feet, and had remained silent, but Van saw him and kicked him again, sending him spiraling down onto his back.

"What do you want?" Blake asked.

Van leaned forward, so close Blake could taste the fresh cigarette on his breath, and for the first time Blake could see his face clearly.

"We want you to lay still, buddy," Van said, pressing his mud-caked boot into Blake's throat. "Nobody fucks with me the way your little girlfriend did. She has to learn that."

He pressed his knee into Blake's chest.

"Ronnie," he said. "You first. Get the girl."

Ronnie laughed and stepped forward. Blake struggled beneath Van's weight, only causing Van to bear down harder.

"They always say that there's one thing sugar and revenge have in common," Ronnie sneered as he leaned down over Greta. "They're both sweet."

He picked her up by her hair and ordered the third assailant to hold her still. The girl held Greta by her arms while Ronnie tilted her chin up to face him.

"Have you ever been kissed, little girl?" Ronnie said, squeezing Greta's lips until they resembled a grimaced pucker. He slapped her hard. "Answer me when I ask you a question!" he bellowed.

Blake quietly eased his pocket knife from his jeans and slid the blade open. Van looked down when he heard the click of the blade locking into place, but it was too late. Blake drove the knife into Van's calf and twisted the handle. Van stumbled backwards, lost his balance, and toppled into the shallow creek with a splash. Blake looked down to the knife in his hand—bloody blade locked into place—and wailed a cry that shook his bones. Van screamed something he couldn't quite make out, but Blake still knew he had to do something before Van got up. He got to his feet and swung a clenched fist hard at Ronnie's face and connected. Ronnie didn't fall, but yelled and staggered backwards. Greta used the heel of her foot to kick the girl holding her repeatedly in the shin. She let go and cried out, "you little bitch!"

Blake and Greta began to run back towards Cass's house, but halted when they heard Van scream.

"Help! Guys! There's something in here with me!"

Startled, they turned to watch.

Van's friends were gathering themselves in the middle of the tiny road, but there was still no sign of Van. Suddenly, he crawled from the dark trench where the shallow creek flowed. He screamed as a figure emerged from the creek behind him brandishing some sort of blunt object. Neither Blake nor Greta could make out what it was.

The figure that had followed Van out of the creek was large, with broad shoulders. It swung the blunt object at one of the three, presumably Ronnie. It sounded like Ronnie when he screamed as he fell to the ground. The figure turned to face the girl, but she cried out and ran deeper into the darkness of Caine's Creek.

Ronnie lay on his back, not moving. Van picked Ronnie up and they scampered away on down the dark roadway.

Blake and Greta had been watching them so intently that they didn't notice the large figure approaching them until it was but a few feet away, taking large, anxious strides.

"Greta," Blake rasped, still out of breath from the weight of Van's knee digging deep into his chest. "Run."

Greta clung to Blake's arm and gasped.

"You kids okay?" The voice was resonate and familiar.

"Cass?" Blake said. He had never noticed just how large Cass was until that moment. "What are you doing out here?"

"I was just... umm..." he stammered. "You kids shouldn't be out so late. Not by yourselves. Bad people out and about. Now, tell me: are you kids okay?"

"I'm fine," Blake said. He sounded stuffy; a thin red line of blood traced his brow. "I think Greta may have twisted her ankle. Cass...."

Cass, who was in the process of picking Greta up in his arms, stopped and looked inquisitively at Blake.

"Thank God you came along when you did," Blake said.

Cass nodded.

"He didn't just come along," Greta said, as Cass scooped her up into his arms. "He was watching over us."

Blake looked at Cass, seeking confirmation that Greta could be right.

"Hush up, girl," Cass said. "They must have hit you pretty hard, didn't they?"

***

It was close to midnight when Cass showed up at Blake's house with the children. He had insisted on seeing them home, seeing as how Greta couldn't walk very well and the folks who had hurt them were presumably still lurking somewhere in the dark, wounded and angry.

The lights were on, so Blake's parents were probably up and worried sick.

Still holding Greta in his arms, Cass knocked on the front door and waited as footsteps approached from the other side. It was Blake's father who answered the door. He stood, stern-faced and slack-jawed when he took in the sight of the battered children in the company of a stranger.

"What's going on here?" Elden said.

"Dad, listen," Blake said.

"Who are you mister?" Elden persisted. "What are you doing with these kids?"

"They got beat up by some other kids," Cass said, walking past Elden and into the living room, placing Greta on the couch. She was sleeping.

"Blake!" Elden shouted. "I told you not to go too far. And what do you do? You run off 'til all hours of the night, and then show up with a beat up girlfriend and a total stranger. I thought you were smarter than that, boy! That little girl's parents are worried sick. And do you have any clue what this has done to your mother?"

"Dad, we were on our way home and some older boys jumped us," Blake said, his voice meek.

"Always excuses, right? You shouldn't have run off in the first place," Elden said. "And who the hell are you?" he said, turning to Cass.

"Well, the name's Cass. But you can think of me as the man who just saved your boy's life." Cass's voice was stern and booming. "I'd show a little appreciation if I were you."

Elden's eyes widened.

"Appreciation?"

"That's right," Cass said. "If I hadn't found 'em when I did, God only knows what may've happened."

"He's telling the truth, Dad," Blake said. "He saved us!"

"If I want your two cents I'll ask for it!" Elden yelled.

Blake shrank away, but a determined fierceness remained in his eyes.

Cass put his hand on Elden's shoulder, and a forefinger to his own lips. "Shhh!" he said. "The little girl is trying to sleep. Turn it down a notch or two."

Elden started to speak, but Cass interjected.

"And try to calm down a little bit. Your boy was just about killed in the middle of the road. Try thanking God he's ok. Show him you love him. Don't yell at him."

Elden started to speak again, but once again was silenced.

"And don't give me that tough love bullshit," Cass said.

He turned and headed for the front door and Blake followed.

"Cass," Blake said. "Thanks again. Sorry about my dad."

"Ain't your fault, kid," Cass said, and walked out the door without looking back.

Elden followed, and called after him.

"Hey, mister!" he said. "Cass, wasn't it?"

Cass turned and looked at Blake's father sternly, as a father eyeing a misbehaving son.

"I'm sorry I got so upset," he said. "We've just recently had a death in the family and I'm a little on edge."

Cass came back up onto the porch and stood in the light spilling from the front door. The light made the features of his face appear jagged and sharp.

"Death in the family?" Cass said. "I'm sorry to hear it." It was the first time Blake had ever heard Cass sound compassionate. "You have my sympathies."

"It was my wife's sister and her husband," Elden said. "They were murdered. Police found their bodies this morning. They'd been there dead for a few weeks at least, and nobody even knew it."

Cass's eyes left Elden and fluttered to the ground. Blake noticed the vacancy that had overtaken Cass's face at the mention of losing a family member.

"So, if I'm edgy," Elden continued, "it's because of that. I've just been so worried about Blake." He tousled Blake's hair.

"Just be thankful for that boy," Cass said, still looking at the ground. Then he looked up at Blake. "He's an alright kid."

"Yeah, I guess he is," Elden said, forcing a smile.

"You folks have a good night," Cass said, and turned to leave.

"You want a ride home?" Elden asked.

"No, thank ya," Cass said. "I'd just as soon walk."

Cass disappeared into the darkness at the edge of the cornfield.

Kenneth S. Harris

Elden turned Blake towards him and examined his wounds.

"Do you know who it was that did this to you?"

"Yeah," Blake said. "Well, two of them anyway. A guy named Van, and another named Ronnie. There was a girl with them, but... ouch!" He grimaced as his father traced the wound on his brow with his finger, checking to see how bad it was. "But I don't know her name."

"We need to get Greta home," Elden said. "I'll call her folks and let them know we're coming."

"Right," Blake said, and rushed to her side.

She looked so peaceful, as though she had spent the evening relaxing in a hammock rather than being assaulted by bullies. Still, even with her cheek glowing with a vibrant red handprint, she was the prettiest girl Blake had ever laid eyes on. He held her hand and kissed it, tears streaming down his face, as he waited for his father to return from calling Greta's parents. In that moment, nothing mattered but her.

13

Blake woke up the next morning sore from head to toe, particularly in his ribs. He'd slept the night through but it had seemed like an eternity, filled with nightmares of the previous evening's events so vivid that it was like living it all over again.

The covers had been tossed aside and he lay on his stomach in nothing but his underwear. He rolled over and swung his legs over the side of the bed and sat up rubbing his eyes.

"You look like hell little cuz. Your mom and dad told me what happened. But other than the bruises, you look about the same as you did the last time I saw you." It was a familiar voice. "Only I believe you were a little shorter, but had more clothes on."

"Jenna!" Blake shouted. He didn't know whether to cower in bed and cover himself or to run to her side to hug her. He settled on a compromise, grabbing the sheet from the floor and wrapping it around his waist, and then flinging himself at her, wrapping his arms around her tiny waste.

She hadn't changed much since Christmas last year. Her hair was slightly longer, still a velvety red like her mother's, and despite a year at college she was still as thin as ever. Jenna was always very popular in school, a cheerleader, track runner and valedictorian. Dianne had looked up to her as a role model for as long as Blake could remember.

Blake looked into her bright green eyes.

"Are you okay?" he asked.

She stroked his cheek and tried to answer, but only an awkward mumble escaped her slightly gaped mouth. Tears streamed down her cheeks and her playful demeanor with which she typically approached her little cousin faded.

"No," she said plainly. "I am so very far from okay. How about you?" She gently brushed the swelling on his face with the side of her thumb.

"Don't worry about me. I'll be fine."

She returned the tight embrace that Blake had offered her. They stood that way until both of their tears had slowed and eventually stopped.

Blake had forgotten how close he and Jenna used to be before she "outgrew him," as his mother had put it when trying to explain why Jenna suddenly had considerably less time for her little cousin. When he was eight years old and she was 16, the two of them were nearly inseparable, particularly in the summer time. Jenna also took up for him if anyone tried to pick on him on the bus. Then she got her driver's license, stopped riding the bus, and made new friends. She "outgrew him," though they still hung out from time to time on weekends and saw each other on holidays.

But any distance that had grown between them was suddenly gone. They walked downstairs together, arms around each other, tears drying on both of their cheeks.

They sat next to each other at breakfast and endured the awkward silence together, exchanging smiles through spoonfuls of eggs. Very little was said.

"How long will you be staying with us, Jenna?" Patty said once. "You're welcome to stay as long as you want."

"Just until after the funeral. I'll need to get back to school. I don't want to get too far behind. Thanks Aunt Patty."

Elden remained silent. He'd never been the type to know what to say in such situations, but Blake knew his heart was going out to Jenna, and that if he could take away her loss he would without a second thought.

"Follow me," Blake said after breakfast. "There's someone I want you to meet."

***

"Blake, we don't blame you. In fact, Greta tells us you got half of your bruises trying to protect her. We still like you very much, so please don't think that we disapprove of you. You're still welcome at our house any time. But maybe you kids should stay a little closer to home for a little while. What do you think?" Vernon told Blake when he and Jenna arrived at his door.

No one had gone to church on that particular Sunday. Vernon invited them both to stay for lunch, though it was still some time away. Throughout the day, if Vernon harbored any resentment, Blake could never tell it. He was his usual, sunny self.

***

Blake hated funerals. He had only been to two in his entire life—one when he was around two years old, much too young to remember, and another at the age of six. Neither was for a family member or even someone he knew, but rather someone his parents knew.

The first night of the viewing began at 7 o'clock for family on Monday, the day after Jenna arrived. Blake had stayed home from school and spent time with her. They looked through old photo albums containing yellowing pictures behind a plastic film and played in the barn like when they were much younger—both activities accompanied by a fair share of tears. It flooded Blake's brain with happy memories, but guilt wasn't far behind. One look at Jenna made him feel ashamed of any form of happiness, even though she was mostly wearing a laborious smile.

Greta came over as soon as she was home from school. Blake and Jenna were sitting in the barn loft, legs dangling from the opened loft doors, and they could see her get off the bus and run towards her house.

"She seems nice. Who'd have thought I'd come home from college and find you with a little girlfriend?" Jenna teased.

"She's not my girlfriend!" Blake said. He could feel himself blushing. But before the words were out of his mouth, Greta had emerged from her house and was running towards them.

"Okay," Jenna said. "I believe you." Soaked in sarcasm.

Blake rolled his eyes at her and then called to Greta. "Hey, how was school?"

"It was a pretty awesome day, actually," she called back. "I have some pretty cool news. But it can wait. How are you feeling?"

She ran into the barn and climbed the dusty, wooden ladder to the loft.

"And Jenna. How are you? I'm so sorry."

Blake was somewhat shocked when Greta wrapped her arms around Jenna and hugged her tightly. Greta still had remnants from Saturday night in her step. It pained Blake to see her hobble with even the slightest limp. It reminded him of the worst day he'd ever experienced. If Cass hadn't showed up when he did, it could have been far worse. But Greta seemed to pay her ankle little mind and carried on in her usual sunny demeanor.

"I'll be okay," Jenna said. "It hurts to know that they're gone, but Blake and I are getting each other through it. I don't know what I would have done without him today."

Blake felt a surge of pride. He thought he had actually been a pest, always at her side throughout the day.

"You're lucky to have this little guy," Jenna said.

Greta hugged her tighter. When they parted Jenna's eyes and cheeks were wet again. She turned to Blake and whispered, "I like her."

Blake smiled.

"I'm going to go get cleaned up for the service," Jenna said, making her way down the ladder to the hay-strewn floor of the barn. She hit the floor with a loud thump and Aphrodite stirred in her stable and snorted.

"Ok, I'll be inside in a minute." He turned to Greta and whispered. "So, what's the big news?"

"You won't believe it," Greta said. "Mom spoke with the principal and told him about what Van did to us the other night. In short, Van Dougherty is no longer a student at Nell Gilman Middle School!"

"What? Really? What happened?"

"Mom called the school and told them what happened, but they said they had no proof that it was Van and Ronnie. Then a teacher caught them holding me against a wall and yelling at me in the lunchroom. When they searched Van's pockets they found a knife on him. They said that was enough and sent him to alternative school!"

"Holy shit! That may be the best news I've heard this year," Blake said.

Greta went home to get ready for the visitation. Blake had told her she didn't have to go if she didn't want to, for as far as he could remember funerals were no fun at all, but she wouldn't hear of it.

Blake dressed in his best khakis and a maroon button-up dress shirt; Jenna wore a black dress that hung just below the knee. When Greta returned she was wearing a charcoal-gray dress with a knitted red shawl. They all left at the same time, Blake's parents driving in front, dressed in their Sunday best; Jenna following closely behind with Blake and Greta on board.

The car ride seemed instantaneous, time seeming to accelerate when approaching an undesirable end. Blake knew everyone involved was dreading what awaited them at the church. He felt a tingling numbness in his legs and a weight on his lungs as they exited Jenna's Corolla and walked towards the building. He took Jenna's hand and squeezed it gently.

Being early for family visitation wasn't exactly a good thing. Blake could see the open caskets from the back of the church and knew it was his aunt and uncle inside. Regardless of the distaste he had for his uncle, Blake felt terrible and could only imagine Jenna felt ten times worse. She walked to the casket and stood over her mother with glistening eyes.

The service was everything Blake remembered funerals to be. He and his family sat up front on a plush couch while a preacher said a few kind words, but eventually got "touched by the spirit" and worked himself into a frenzy of prayer. Blake couldn't help but roll his eyes and hope that no one noticed. He found the mention of heaven and hell, and whether or not his departed family members were damned, to be distasteful and disrespectful. He squeezed Jenna's hand throughout the service.

He heard Jenna crying that night as he lay in his bed trying to sleep. He wanted to go to her, but figured she could use the time to be alone, get it all out of her system. If his parents had been the ones to die, he would want to cry, and he would likely want to do it alone.

The second day of funeral services were much like the first, but with a slightly larger crowd, many of which Blake had never seen before. These people looked rougher than Blake had expected. He'd heard stories about his uncle's "wild side," as his mother liked to call it, but had never met any of the folks he used to run with. None of them spoke to the family. In fact, they hardly paid Jenna, Blake or his parents any mind at all.

The third day was the day everyone dreaded the most, especially Jenna. Blake couldn't settle his mind on seeing someone being lowered into the ground. They arrived at the cemetery around 2 o'clock in the afternoon, after a brief sermon preached by Reverend Statler, a good friend of Blake's parents. Contrary to the common assumption, burials are not always plagued by rain; the sun was shining that day, beaming down between puffy white clouds. Jenna's car had led the funeral march, directly behind the hearse and Sheriff Bryant's car, followed closely by Blake's parents and everyone else. Blake, Jenna, and Greta walked on to the burial site—two large, gaping holes in the ground with mounds of dirt next to them—and waited as the pallbearers, including Blake's dad, carried the coffins up the hill.

When the coffins finally began to lower into the ground, Jenna and Blake's mother burst out in sobs, clinging to one another. Greta held Blake's hand, but he never cried, just looked on with an odd acceptance tainted by a growing fear that he too would one day die.

"I need to take a walk," Blake said.

Greta nodded and accompanied him back down the hill towards where the vehicles were parked. As they descended the grassy slope, Blake saw a familiar-looking figure standing in the shade of a tree that overhung the cemetery's chain-link fence. Looking much the way he did just a few nights ago, Cass looked on towards the burial proceedings up the hill, not noticing Blake and Greta.

"Cass? What are you doing here?" Blake said.

Cass looked at him, his face startled and lacking color. He was dressed in a gray suit with a white dress-shirt underneath. The sleeves were a good two inches short for his arms and the shoulders appeared stretched across his broad frame, ready to pop should he inhale too deeply. His hair was combed and parted in the middle, but his stubble had grown into a thick, short mess of beard.

"Boy? Is that you? Why are you ... ?" Blake ran up to him, Greta following closely behind. "Do you know the folks up there?" he said, nodding to the funeral.

"Yeah," Blake said. "That's my aunt and uncle."

"I'm real sorry," Cass stammered, obviously unsure what to say or how to say it. "I'm real sorry to hear that."

"Thanks," Blake said. "Did you know them?"

"Who? Your aunt and uncle? Nope, I sure didn't. I just like to pay my respects when somebody passes on."

"Why pay them from way down here?" Greta asked. "Why not come on up the hill with everybody else? I'm sure no one would mind. Right, Blake?"

"Sure, nobody would mind," Blake said.

"I like to pay my respects from a distance," Cass said. "I got my reasons."

"Like what?" Greta asked.

"Well, first off, I didn't think I'd know anybody up there. I didn't want to seem like I was gettin' in the way. Second, funerals make me a little sick at my stomach."

"I understand that," Blake said.

The funeral party had begun descending the hill. Jenna was way out in front. Blake could tell she was still sobbing even in the distance, her head hung and her hands covering part of her face.

"Well, I gotta run," Cass said. "You all be good."

"Wait one minute, Cass," Blake said. "I want you to meet Jenna."

"Boy, I don't really have time," he replied.

"Come on! It'll only take a second." He turned and shouted, "Jenna!" and motioned her towards them.

"Hey, Blake," she said, sniffling, her eyes red and puffy. "Who's your friend?" She stood next to Blake and put a heavy arm across his shoulders.

"This is Cass," Blake said. "Cass, this is my cousin, Jenna."

"Cousin?" Cass said. "You mean that's your parents?" he added, pointing up the hill. Jenna nodded. "I'm so sorry," Cass said. "So sorry."

"Thank you," Jenna said. "I never imagined losing ... "

"I hate to, but I gotta run," Cass said. "You all take care." And he turned and walked down the path and passed the cars in a hurry.

"Your friend seems like an odd one," Jenna said, her voice rough from crying.

"Yeah, but he's an alright guy," Blake said. "He saved our skins the other night." He pointed to his fading bruises.

"Yeah, thank God for small favors, I guess," Jenna said.

14

Jenna left the next day to return to school, promising she would call and visit often. She, Blake and Greta had stayed up late telling stories and reminiscing about happier times. Before she left, Jenna and Blake agreed that they needed to be closer than ever now. It was a pact Blake planned to honor.

Blake and Greta started spending afternoons in the swing on Greta's front porch, or in the barn loft at Blake's farm. Their time together had become less adventurous due to being bound to the area between their homes, but had also become far more valuable. Blake would hold Greta's hand and talk about what they would do when they were no longer restricted to home. He even taught her some details about farming, like cleaning chicken coups, gathering eggs, milking the cow, and picking green beans.

One time they got to leave the farm with Charlotte to return the library books, but not until Greta had read the entirety of *Afternoonls*.

Days and then weeks passed slowly, filled with school, homework, and races through rows of towering corn stalks; an autumn chill had taken to the air, turning the lush greenery of Hemingford into a spectrum of warm color. They both kept their guard up at school, Ronnie and the unknown boy were hell bent on getting back at them, especially after Van got sent to alterative school.

Blake wondered if Greta had ever witnessed anything like a farm community in the fall. He wondered if even the most beautiful tree would stand out in the city. He remembered a few trips he had made to Cincinnati with his father when he was younger. He couldn't recall any trees, but he was sure they were there. All he could remember were buildings; a lot of buildings, and streets.

Blake was sure Greta would make the most of the fall, just like she did everything else. But with Halloween approaching, Blake was determined that he and Greta had to find a way to get back in the adventure game. Halloween was Blake's favorite holiday. It pained him terribly to think of a Halloween spent at home and not out wondering the streets in search of sweets, dressed in a ghoulish costume, running from older kids apt to play childish pranks, and thus preying on younger kids with pranks of his own. However, he didn't think Van and his crew had *childish* pranks in mind.

Step one, talk it over with Greta, he thought. *Maybe she'll have a plan. She can talk me in to just about anything. Maybe she can do the same with her folks.*

Since being confined to playing at home, it had become a tradition for Blake and Greta to meet after school in the corn fields, third row from the back. On a particular Thursday, they met in their usual spot to plan a way to get out into the world again.

Blake began the brainstorming process.

"What about Cass? He's an adult, right? A grown man. What if he would meet us somewhere and let us walk with him?"

"I'm not sure," Greta said. "I don't think spending evenings with us would be Cass's cup of tea. Not to mention our parents don't really know him that well."

"You're probably right. But what if it was just one night?"

"Just one night?"

"Halloween! Please tell me they have Halloween in the city!" he said, sarcastically.

"Yes, of course we do."

"Not like we have it here, I bet," he said wearing a proud smile.

"What's so special about Halloween in this town? What do people do differently?"

"It's not what the *people* do," Blake said. "It's the town itself. The whole place lights up. You see carved pumpkins and tacky decorations everywhere! And fodder shocks! And the best part, the Fall Festival! I've never missed a single year. And I'm not about to miss this one."

"I have to admit," Greta said. "I don't think I've ever seen you this excited about ... well ... anything. If you say it's so great, I supposed the absolute least I can do is check it out."

"Yeah!" Blake said. "Now, the question is: How do we pull this off?"

"There's a chance my parents may let me go," she said. "Yours too. It's a supervised event, right?"

"Yeah, it all happens at the grade school. That way we wouldn't have to ask Cass to go with us. The whole building looks like a carnival. Games and candy everywhere! And out back, where the fifth grade buildings are there's a haunted house!"

"It sounds pretty cool," Greta said. "I just can't believe they finally found a good use for a school building."

***

The next morning, Blake waited for the bus with his head hung low like the fog about his feet. The chill in the air was typical of early October.

"Well, at least I have good news," Greta said regretfully, as she ran to meet him. "I take it your parents weren't as easy to convince as mine?"

"Apparently not," Blake said. "They just kept saying it was too soon and all. And truthfully, I get where they're coming from. Everybody's pretty freaked out about what happened. And I know Mom misses Aunt Dory. Nobody really misses her asshole husband."

"Was he really that bad?"

"Take bad and add 10 to it. I have no idea what Aunt Dory saw in him." He paused. "Mostly, I'm worried sick about Jenna, being so far away and all."

"I'm sure she'll call if she needs anything."

"Yeah, I reckon she will."

Blake heard the bus stop and the door hiss open just down the road at Hayley Adams' house. He and Greta both turned to look at it.

"I get why they don't want me going too far from the house. I really do," he said, still looking at the approaching bus in the distance. "But life has to go on, doesn't it?"

"Sure it does," Greta said. "They just don't want you to get hurt. Especially after what happened with Van and his friends."

"Yeah, what I wouldn't give to bust him up good," Blake said.

"Well, you'll probably get the chance. I imagine they're not too happy with us."

"I expect you're right. If only they weren't so big, I'd be looking forward to it more," Blake grinned.

The bus made its way through the morning fog. But while Blake was laughing on the outside, he kept thinking that he'd die if he had to, fighting Van and his thugs, if it meant protecting Greta. Every time he looked at her he could still picture the bright red handprint on her face.

15

October was riddled with spooks and ghosts. They seemed to be lurking everywhere: in English class, they read *The Legend of Sleepy Hollow* by Washington Irving, and once they had completed the short story, they watched the movie as well; in History, Ms. Kemper had reserved the Salem Witch Trials to be their topic of study for the majority of the month.

Truly, Halloween even made school interesting; even for those who were a bit harder to intrigue in the classroom.

Blake had seen no sign of Van Dougherty since he left Nell Gilman for alternative school. He still thought about that night often, could still smell the damp pines muddled with the iron stench of a crushed nose, and could still hear Greta struggle against their assailants.

It's sort of funny to think Van would want to pay us back, Blake thought. *What've we done? It was us that had to walk around looking like what was left of a car wreck.*

Van and his buddies started it; Cass had finished it. But Blake and Greta still may end up paying for it.

Blake and Greta went about their daily routine, day after day, trying their best not to think about Van. Their days were riddled with orange, black, purple and red decorations. Average colors, yes. But during Halloween, they became the colors of "ghastly." This was truly Blake's favorite time of the year, and he wasn't about to fill his days with sickened worry because of an ignorant bully.

***

October passed quickly with no sign of Van, but also very little sign of Cass. The only time they had heard from him was in a letter that he'd tacked to a tree that stood to the side of Blake's house. Blake could see it from his window when he woke up. The contrast of the white page against the burning autumn colors struck him immediately. The page curled up at the corners from the persistent gusts of a gentle breeze.

The letter was damp when Blake pulled it down, but still readable. Cass wrote in jagged scrawls:

> *Blake, you and your little girlfriend come see me some time. I get lonesome up here all by myself. And don't worry about them bigger kids. They shouldn't be bothering you. And if they do, I'll thump em again.*
> *- Cass*

Blake found two things about the letter comforting: One being that Cass had promised protection against Van and his pals. Two, that he had called Greta his "little girlfriend."

Blake, in a fit of joy, had taken the letter up to his room and hidden it inside his pillow case.

He and Greta had considered talking to Cass before the Fall Festival, perhaps inviting him along. Van would certainly think twice before bugging them if Cass were with them. He even went so far as to nail a reply letter to the same tree where Cass had left his, asking him to come. Unfortunately, Cass never found it. It turned to mush after the first rain.

As far as getting Blake to the festival, the plan was simple: Blake would say he is spending the evening at Greta's house, then he would simply ride to the festival with Greta's parents. Greta's parents, being the carefree folks that they were, would drop them off and pick them up later. After all, how could Blake's parents mind if he rode with the well-trusted neighbors?

His parents agreed to let him spend the evening with Greta if he promised he'd be home around 11. But after careful consideration, he decided not to ask about the festival. In this case, it would just have to be best to assume.

Blake left his house around 6:30 that evening and headed to Greta's through the corn. It was a Friday and he'd only been home from school a little while, but it was long enough to get his costume together. The sunset made the sky look like fire, yet the ground held onto the dull colors of dusk.

When he came through the door, Greta hugged him tightly.

"Where's your costume?" she asked.

He held up a paper grocery bag and grinned. "Couldn't risk mom and dad asking too many questions."

Greta was already in full Halloween attire: a flowing black dress with sleeves down to the heel of her hands and a purple sash. She smiled and donned a black veil, completing the costume.

"What are you supposed to be?" Black asked.

"Isn't it obvious? I'm a tasteful, yet slightly disturbed, widow of the 19th century."

"I see," Blake said, raising an eyebrow.

"Go get changed!" Greta urged. "You've built this up too much. I don't want to be late."

Blake hurried to the downstairs bathroom to change into his costume. He entered the room as a normal 12-year-old boy, but exited 30 minutes later in silence. He was wearing black slacks, a red long-sleeved shirt, black suspenders and a messenger's cap, cocked to one side. His face was painted white, but his lips were black and two thin black lines ran up and down from his eyes.

"A mime! What gave you the idea for that?"

"The way Annie's always telling me to shut up. I figure this is the perfect costume, and perhaps lifestyle, if I ever wanted to get on her good graces. But of course, I don't." He smiled.

"Wow, Blake!" Vernon said. "Didn't expect such a costume. Nice job!"

"Thanks, Mr. Wills."

"Come on, kids," Charlotte said from the living room. "Let's get going."

They both sat in the backseat on the way to the festival. Charlotte shined over their costumes and couldn't quit raving over their grandeur.

When they pulled into the school's parking lot, only a sliver of red sun remained. The place looked pretty crowded, some cars dropping children off, others parking in the crowded lot. Some people were in costume, some weren't.

"You kids be careful. And have a great time!" Charlotte said as they exited the car.

"We will, Mom! Thanks for the lift."

The inside of the school looked familiar to Blake. He had gone to this grade school when he was younger and every year the Fall Festival transforms the place into an amicable tribute to his favorite holiday.

The school was heavily decorated with orange, purple and black streamers. The large room that served as both auditorium and cafeteria was filled with snack tables lined with punch bowls, cups of soft-drinks, treat bags, fruit and more. In the back, children were flinging basketballs at a row of hoops beneath a large black and orange sign: "Make 10 and Win a Prize!"

Blake glanced at Greta. Her mouth was hanging open in awe. Being the new kid in town, she had never even been inside this school. But Blake could imagine that most grade schools were the same, and to see any school in such splendor would have that effect.

"I told ya," Blake said.

"This is great!"

"Just wait until you see the rest!"

"How much more awesome can it get?" Greta beamed.

"I'll show you!"

Blake took her hand and they scampered through the crowd and exited the cafeteria through a set of double doors at the far end. The hallway was much in the same fashion. It smelled of sweet Halloween: cinnamon and pumpkin, candy corn, and steaming apple cider. The hall was even more crowded than the cafeteria.

This particular hallway had doors that opened onto the cafeteria on one side, and a rectangular courtyard on the other. Blake and Greta stepped out into the courtyard, stars and moon both peering down through the open ceiling. It was lit with jack-o-lanterns and strands of purple and orange lights. The walls were lined with tables containing games, packets of candy, and bowls of punch and apple cider. They each paid for a cup of cider and stood watching as a young boy, probably around the age of seven, threw suction darts at a dart board. The next table down had a large tub filled with water and floating plastic ducks. A young girl dressed as a lady bug and her mother were lifting up the ducks to try to match three sets of pictures.

"There's more!" Blake said.

They returned to the hall, rounded the corner and went through another set of double doors.

"This is one of my favorite parts," Blake said. "This hall is filled with classrooms. But tonight, every classroom has a pretty cool game in it."

"Blake, we didn't have anything like this in the city. This is amazing!"

"I know! I love it! I look forward to it every year. I've saved up some money so we can play all the games we want. But on one condition."

"What condition?"

"We save the haunted house for last. You know, like a big finale to the night."

"Sounds good! Let's get started!"

Blake showed Greta around the school and they played various games throughout the evening. Greta's favorite room was the library, where the school's librarian

Mrs. Belcher sat reading spooky stories to a crowd of huddled children dressed in costumes. Blake liked it too. It stoked his interest in storytelling and twisted it together with his favorite holiday. It didn't take Greta long to talk him into sticking around to hear a few. They trick-or-treated to all the classrooms, occasionally playing games. They ate candy and drank punch. But at last, when Blake noticed it was getting close to 10 o'clock, he said: "We only have about 30 minutes left before your mom gets back, let's head on out to the haunted house."

"Sure thing," Greta said. "Mom probably wouldn't mind if we were a few minutes late."

***

"Are you scared?" Blake asked, as they made their way to the back of the school.

"Are you kidding?" Greta said. "We have haunted houses in the city, and I'd be willing to bet they're a lot scarier than this one."

"We'll see about that," Blake said.

The haunted house was always in one of the fifth-grade buildings, located behind the school. They were a tiny row of yellow buildings, separate from the large schoolhouse, no doubt built as an afterthought as the school grew and more space was needed. They each had tiny wooden decks with a couple steps leading up. It was easy to pick out which was the haunted house. Most lay dormant with dark windows. However, one particular building's windows glowed with a soft purple light and occasionally snapped with a brilliant flash of white light, almost like lightning. Thick, synthetic fog poured from the open door.

Blake and Greta climbed the steps and walked to the door. They each paid one dollar and went inside. The lady who took their money was Mrs. Emily Wallace, Blake's fifth-grade teacher. He was almost hurt that she didn't recognize him, but then he remembered he was hidden under a thick layer of make-up.

They were waiting in line with a few other children and a few parents for the tour to start when Blake heard a familiar voice.

"This is kid's stuff. Look how lame this is." Followed by a shredding noise.

"Now you boys quit that or I'll have to ask you to leave," said Mrs. Wallace.

"Did you hear that?" Blake said.

"Hear what?"

"Those boys outside talking to Mrs. Wallace."

"Yeah, they sound like idiots."

"I agree," Blake said. "But listen closer. They sound like very specific idiots."

Greta put a finger to her pursed lips and turned an ear towards the door. Her eyes widened.

"It's Van!" she said.

"I know! And we have to walk past them to get out."

"What are we going to do?" Greta whispered, sounding panicked.

"Pull your veil down," Blake said. "Maybe they won't see your face."

"What about you?" she said, pulling her veil down as low as it would go.

"Let's hope the face paint is enough to make them not recognize me."

The entire atmosphere of the tiny waiting hall changed when the boys entered, as if everyone became uncomfortable all at once. Blake stood quietly with his back to the boys, hoping to blend in with the other children. He could hear their voices, which delivered him a vivid reminder of all the vile things they had said to him and Greta that night. His blood felt like it was simmering. His hands clenched into tight fists.

"Stay in front of me," he whispered to Greta.

A lady dressed as a witch with a pale green face and long black hair came out into the hallway. She said in a raspy voice: "Good evening, children. It is now time to enter the house of horror! Where terror awaits and nothing can keep you safe. Not even your mommy and daddy!"

A few younger kids closer to the front of the line began to sob, but the lady didn't break character. She held back the door.

"Enter, if you dare!"

The line began to move, but Blake's mind wasn't on the terror that lay ahead. He was more focused on the terror that stood just a few feet behind him. Greta got in front of Blake like he had asked her to and they fell in line with the rest of the group entering the haunted house.

Even once they were inside in the darkness, with people dressed in ghoulish costumes, coffins lining the walls, cobweb-consumed candelabras sitting upon dusty furniture and lights flashing intensely, Blake could still hear Van's voice talking about how lame everything was and how anybody who enjoyed such a thing was an idiot. He was pretty sure he could make out Ronnie's voice too.

He ventured a quick glance behind him, and sure enough it was Ronnie who accompanied Van, along with a third person, most likely the unknown girl from the night Cass had saved them.

Van was laughing, but he stopped laughing when he saw Blake. His expression changed into a foul grimace and he pointed, alerting his friends.

Blake heard him say: "It's that little punk! Let's get him!"

Blake's heart nearly stopped. He grabbed Greta's hand.

"We've gotta go now! We've gotta get out of here!"

They ran past everyone in front of them, carelessly pushing past people who exclaimed: "Hey watch it kid!" and "Where do you think you're going?"

They turned the first corner of the haunted house, which led them down a slender dark hallway. A man wearing a wolf mask jumped out in front of them and howled loudly, but they simply ran on past him paying him little mind.

Blake couldn't see Van behind them, but that didn't mean he had given up. It would likely take a lot to make Van give up. The haunted house was dark inside, with only the occasional flash of brilliant light to showcase the intended terror. Blake paid it no mind, being too focused on the unintended terror that pursued them.

On the other side of the hallway they could barely make out an open room with a row of coffins lining one wall and another sitting atop a table with a skirt reaching from the top of the table to the floor. For a moment, Blake considered hiding, either inside one of the standing coffins or underneath the draped table, but decided against it when he thought of Van stopping to search the area and how terrible it would be if he found them.

Instead, he took Greta's hand tightly and headed towards the backdoor. Hiding seemed favorable, because he knew he and Greta couldn't outrun Van and his buddies.

They exited the haunted fifth-grade classroom onto the tiny deck. It was actually lighter outside thanks to the moon than it had been inside.

Blake leaped the railing and stumbled to the ground, which was much further away than he expected.

"Blake, are you okay?" Greta took the steps, walked to the side of the deck and knelt beside him where he lay sprawled in the wet evening grass.

He took her hand and was about to lead her around the side of the building when he noticed a hole in the deck's underpinning.

"Yeah, in here!"

His adrenaline was high and his fingers fumbled with the lose underpinning. At last, he pulled it back and motioned Greta inside. Apprehensively, she crawled under the deck and Blake followed. They huddled in the darkness and scurried back away from the opening. He put his arm around her protectively and lowered his cheek onto the top of her head. The space beneath the deck was damp and small, but it would have to do.

It was quiet for a moment and Blake entertained the idea that Van had decided to leave them alone. But clumsy, angry footsteps on the deck above broke the silence.

"Which way'd they go?" Ronnie said.

"How the hell should I know?" Van answered.

Blake could see their feet drag across the paved walkway after they jumped down from the deck. They lingered. Blake held his breath.

"We'll get 'em," Van said. "I'll go this way. Ronnie, that way. And Katie, you go that way."

"Alright, sounds like a plan," the girl's voice said.

The sounds of their feet departed in various directions, but Blake and Greta sat perfectly still until they could no longer hear them. Blake stuck his head out first and peered around. He saw no sign of their foes and came out, followed closely by Greta. She was shaking terribly. She sat on the grass with her arms curled around her knees and took deep breaths.

"You alright?" Blake asked.

"Yeah, I just hate, hate—" she gasped. "I hate closed spaces."

Blake's first thought was *wow, Greta is afraid of something*, but thought it wouldn't be right to say it. Instead, he put his hand on her shoulder and said, "I'm sorry."

"Not your fault," Greta said a little steadier. "It got us away from those guys, so I say good job. Besides, you didn't know."

"Your veil is gone," Blake said. He hadn't even noticed while resting his cheek on her soft hair.

Greta eyed him with a look that playfully said, "as if it matters."

They sat for a moment while Greta's breathing returned to normal. But Blake had troubled thoughts.

"Van called that girl Katie." He sounded troubled. "I think I know her."

"Really?" she said, still sucking long drags of the cool night air. "Who was it?"

"Katie Greene. She used to hang out with Dianne with they were little. It couldn't be though. She was always such a nice person."

"Don't let it bother you. It probably wasn't her. But let's worry about it later," Greta said, getting to her feet and eyeing a watch that rested just beneath the sleeve of her dress. "Mom is supposed to pick us up in about five minutes. Let's just get back to the front of the school without running into those assholes."

"Good plan," Blake said. "Now, let's see if we can pull it off."

They hugged the side of the main school building, concealed mostly by the hedges and shadows, until they reached the front corner of the school. There were plenty of cars picking up kids and plenty still parked in the parking lot—no sign of Van, Ronnie or Katie, likely the Katie that Blake had always valued as a friend, or at the very least, a friend of his sister's.

"There's mom!" Greta said.

They both ran towards the black sedan.

"There they are!" It was Van. His voice was replaced by a frantic shuffle of hurrying feet.

Blake turned towards the source of the voice and saw Van running from the other end of the school down the sidewalk. There were quite a few people outside, but not enough to stop Van from pushing and shoving his way ever closer.

Greta screamed! Katie had emerged from the other side of the building and grabbed her by the arm. Katie Greene. Blake thought he noticed a look of apology in her eyes. But he didn't care. Greta hit her as hard as she could in the plump of her round nose. Katie stumbled backwards, letting go of her.

Blake expected retaliation, but Katie just stood there holding her bleeding nose with sparkling, wet eyes. Van came upon them in a hurry, but by this point Charlotte had noticed the scuffle.

"What are you doing? Stay away from them!" she bellowed from the driver's seat through the rolled-down passenger's window.

Blake opened the car door, but as Greta was getting in, Van grabbed her hair, apparently disregarding her mother's presence. Greta shrieked. She reached back and grabbed at the sides of Van's head. He screamed and let her go. She plunged into the car and Blake followed quickly.

"Get us out of here!" Blake screamed. "Those guys are crazy!"

Charlotte drove away as soon as the door was closed.

"Were those the kids you had trouble with before?" she asked furiously. "Nobody treats my child that way!"

Blake and Greta nodded.

"I've already took it up with the principle," she said. "Maybe it's time to talk to the police! Are you kids okay?"

"Yeah, we're fine, Mom," Greta said. "Just a little shook up."

Blake admired her courage and determination. He smiled at her, but her lip was quivering. It was then that he noticed she was holding a tiny silver earring in the center of her bloody palm.

"I think Van will want this back," she said.

16

"I think we could use a quiet evening indoors," Greta said. "Did your parents ever find out you went to the Fall Festival?"

"Nope, thank God," Blake said. "And I agree. An evening inside. Just you, me and Joe Bob Briggs."

The television—Joe Bob's *Monster Vision*—flashed in sporadic bursts of bright light, glowing on their faces in the dark room. Joe Bob promised to deliver nothing but classic horror films into the wee morning hours. The house smelled of buttered popcorn and candles heating the inside hulls of freshly-carved jack-o-lanterns.

"I love it when Halloween is on a weekend," Blake said. "We can stay up late and not worry about school the next day."

"Agreed."

"What did you do with Van's earring?"

"I hid it," she said. "I'm not sure how Mom would react if she found out. She called the police and everything."

"Wow. Well, maybe they'll leave us alone for a change."

"Maybe, but I don't know. Van seemed more pissed than ever, and ripping his earring out probably didn't help the way he feels about us. Or *me*, I should say."

"Good point. But don't beat yourself up. That guy has been giving me hell since first grade."

Kenneth S. Harris

Blake and Greta sat on the couch watching *Night of the Living Dead*, the first in the *Monster Vision Movie Marathon*, followed by *Spider Baby* and last but not least, *Halloween*. On the table in front of them sat a large bowl of hot popcorn—Blake had brought the dried kernels from home, farm fresh—and an even larger bowl of trick-or-treat candy for any visitors they may have. Kids who were out doing what Blake would normally be doing.

Kids in costumes came and went. Charlotte typically answered the door with a great smile, candy bowl in hand. But a couple of times Blake and Greta answered the door, holding their breath until they saw that their visitor was not Van, Ronnie or Katie. But then again, coming to Greta's house would probably take more guts than Van had.

Almost at the end of *Spider Baby*, Blake chanced sliding his arm around Greta's shoulder. She didn't seem to mind, but rather, slid down comfortably into the nook of his arm. Blake held his breath and his arm remained rigid until he realized Greta seemed at ease.

When Blake left to walk home, about halfway through *Halloween*, Greta walked him to the door. It was a little after midnight. They stood in silence for a moment, but then Greta took both of his hands and kissed him on the lips so fast and without warning that Blake barely had time to kiss back.

His eyes grew wide and when he started to speak Greta held her hand up to his mouth.

"Not a word, Blake," she said. "That was for being the best friend I've ever had. And I like you. A lot. Now go on home. I'll see you tomorrow."

She was blushing, her cheeks a bright red.

"Good night," Blake said, smiling.

She went back inside and he left down the tall steps of the porch. He considered this the best Halloween he could remember. The smile on his face felt permanent. However, it faded when he saw the tattered remains of Greta's black veil laying on the bottom step.

He picked it up and looked around quickly. He saw nothing. But without doubt, Van had been there.

17

Monday morning felt like November, cold and foggy with a light frost on the grass. Blake walked down his driveway, eager to talk to Greta, yet nervous. She had kissed him. He imaged they would continue being close friends as they always had, only they may kiss again or hold hands. Typical boyfriend and girlfriend stuff. Too many questions were racing about in his mind. He pushed them away, worrying about a simple truth: he had never felt nervous when approaching the school bus stop and Greta before. Perhaps everything would change. He just didn't know.

He had talked to her on the phone yesterday, but only for a little while. Elden had changed his "no chores on Sunday" policy in light of getting in the last of the year's corn harvest. Blake had been busy all day helping his father; Greta had gone shopping with her parents.

He reached the end of the driveway and stood in knee-deep fog waiting for the bus. Was he early? Usually Greta was waiting on him when he reached the roadside. But not today.

Maybe she had gotten her parents to drive her to school because she didn't want to face Blake. Maybe she regretted kissing him and would just avoid him from here on out?

Blake peered hard towards Greta's house hoping to see her come running out of the fog, just a few minutes late. But the fog grew thick in the distance and he could barely make out the tips of the leaning cornstalks.

Instead of Greta, the school bus came rumbling towards him in the distance. For some reason, Blake panicked. The bus passed Greta's house without even slowing down. And why would it? Irvin was used to picking Blake and Greta up together either at the end of Blake's driveway or about midway through the length of the cornfield.

The bus stopped in front of him and the doors slid open.

Blake stepped on and glanced down the aisles looking for Greta. She wasn't there.

"Irvin, is Greta on the bus?" he asked.

"No siree. Maybe she's sick today."

"Maybe." Blake stepped off the bus. "I'm going to run down to her house and check on her. I'll get mom to give me a lift to school."

For a moment, he thought Irvin was going to insist that he get on the bus, that he couldn't have kids ditching school on his account. But he just said, "Okie dokie, chief. I'll see you this evenin'." And the bus drove away leaving the stink of exhaust to mingle with the fog.

Blake's heart was pounding in his chest. He could almost taste it. He pushed concerns of irrationality out of his head. He was terrified and couldn't think of anything else. Greta had never missed a day of school, at least not since he had known her. He ran towards Greta's house, hoping he would soon find out that Greta was safe in her bed with nothing more than the sniffles.

He tripped and stumbled slightly and only stopped for a moment to look back at what had disrupted his footing. When he saw what it was, he fell hard to the ground. The grass, sharp with frost, stung his bare hands as he tumbled and slid to a halt. It seemed so surreal. Like his feet suddenly decided to stop moving or even hold him up. It was Greta's backpack lying on the ground, as shocking as sudden sun on a cloudy day.

He crawled towards it and picked it up. The zipper was broken and the pack was half-opened. Terrified, he surveyed the area. His eyes welled up and stung in the morning cold when he saw her. He screamed, hardly conscious of any action.

She was lying in a hump just shy of being concealed by the cornfield in the tiny ditch that separated the grass from the corn. She lay face down beneath the fog like it was a blanket. The back of her shirt was split open and Blake could just make out several scratches on her back. Her pants and underwear were pulled down almost to her knees. Her skin was smeared with dirt, but otherwise as perfect as porcelain, setting itself apart from the horrid scene. There was blood in her hair that hadn't even had time to dry. She wasn't moving.

Still screaming, Blake ran to her side and rolled her over. She whimpered slightly but her eyes remained closed. He took off his coat and spread it over her nakedness, horrified. He held her head to his chest and screamed, ignoring the bitter cold biting at his arms.

Elden came running down the driveway and saw them in the distance.

"Blake!" he shouted. "What's wrong? What happened?"

He approached the children and stopped dead when he took in the scene. He knelt beside them and said, "We have to get her to the hospital. What in the hell happened here?"

Elden carried Greta to her parents' house, Blake running ahead of him and ringing the doorbell fervently before his father even reached the bottom of the steps. Charlotte answered the door in tan slacks and a dress jacket, still fixing an earring to her ear. Her expression changed the moment she saw Greta, her hands shaking as she took her daughter into her arms. In panic, Charlotte took her into the house, called for Vernon and they all headed for the hospital. Blake rode with Greta and her family and his father followed swiftly in his pickup. He told them how he had found her and Charlotte wailed so loud it seemed to shake Blake's bones.

For Blake, the trip seemed almost instantaneous. They got in the car, then it was time to get out. He had stopped crying and followed Vernon, who was carrying Greta, until they told him he'd have to wait outside.

He and his father sat in the waiting room for what seemed like an eternity. So many thoughts were in Blake's head. So many, he didn't trust any of them. Everything he looked at had an edge to it. An edge that could cut that he'd never noticed before. For the first time in his life, the world seemed truly evil and it had landed its wicked hand on Greta.

He hadn't had a rational thought since setting eyes on Greta's crumpled body. But sitting in the waiting room with nothing to do but think, rationale came. *Van did this,* he thought. *Had to be.*

So caught up in his thoughts, he didn't notice Greta's father come out into the waiting area and sit down next to them.

"Is she okay?" Elden asked.

Blake looked up.

"She's going to be okay, thank God," Vernon said. "The doctors think someone tried to—"

He looked nervously at Blake and then to his father.

"No secrets here," Elden said. "Tell us what happened."

"They think someone tried to rape her." He started crying in spite of obvious effort not to. He hid his face with one hand, his body convulsing with each sob. "My little girl." He took deep breaths and Blake came to his side and put his arm around him. "She got away. But, but, when she did. She. She fell and hit her head. Blake must have scared whoever. Whoever it was off. Thank you so much Blake for getting there when you did."

He burst in to wails. The false light, the stench of disinfectant, it all seem to welcome uncontrolled cries. Blake's hands trembled with such ferocity that he could feel it in the length of his arms and in his chest. But he never moved his hand's from Vernon's shoulder. All the while though, he was thinking of how much and how severely Van Dougherty would pay.

***

It was almost one o'clock before Blake was allowed back to see her. And even then, him not being family and all, Greta had to demand to see him. She simply stated she would not eat until she saw Blake. The doctors reluctantly gave in since Vernon had no objection.

He came into the room and stood beside her bed. Looking at him, Greta's eyes filled with tears and one skirted the curve of her cheek. She sat up and tugged lightly at his shirt. He hugged her, forgetting about the nurse and her father in the room.

"Blake, it was awful. The things he tried to do to me. And I couldn't stop him."

Blake stroked her hair, noticing the blood was gone—replaced by thick, white gauze—and her hair was silky and smooth. "It's okay. You're alright and that's all that matters."

He had heard his father say that to him before when he was younger. He had fallen out of the barn loft after being forbidden to go up there. "You're too little," Elden had said. "You'll get up there and get hurt." But when the dust had cleared and the scrapes were cleaned, his father had said those exact words.

Something like this would grow someone up in a hurry, Blake reckoned. This thought, coupled with what had happened to Greta, made him cry. But he kept it silent, letting her fresh-washed hair catch his tears.

He pulled back and looked at her. Her face was red and streaked. The only addition of color to the otherwise bleak, white room. The television played silently in a corner close to the ceiling.

"You're the only one who's ever called me pretty," she said.

"Greta, you're the prettiest girl I've ever seen. Always will be," he said without hesitation. "I was so scared. Still am to be honest."

"I don't know who did it," she said. "He came up behind me and grabbed me." Again, tears. "He was tall and had a deep voice. But I didn't even see him when I tried to get away. I was too scared to look! Then I fell and the next thing I knew I was in my dad's arms." She cried on. "And I lost my necklace," she said, groping at her bare neck where the owl had rested for going on three months.

"I'll make you another one," Blake choked out, the words getting caught up in the heavy spit in his throat.

Vernon came to her side. Together, they held her until the sobs were gone and she was asleep again, which took the better part of an hour.

Elden, who had patiently stayed in the waiting room, practically had to *make* him leave around 2:30. Blake wrote Greta a note and left it on her bedside, promising to come back the next day. He even kissed her forehead, not so much as giving a thought to someone objecting. He felt something for her, stronger than ever, that he simply could not explain.

All the way home, Blake hadn't said a word, just looked absently out the truck window, until his father broke the silence.

"Did she say she got a look at who it was?"

"No."

"Shew," Elden said. "It ain't safe for nobody no more."

18

As soon as they got home, Blake ran to his room after assuring his dad he would be okay, and that he just needed some time alone. As soon as the door shut, he crawled out his window and onto the slight overhang of the house, and then gently eased himself down onto the ground. Relieved no one saw, he hurried towards his bicycle. He knew about where Van lived. If he rode fast enough, he could reach Caine's Creek before dark.

He rode faster than he believed possible, ignoring the dull ache forming in his thighs and calves. The sun was still burning bright, in contradiction to the nip of cold stinging his face and neck, when he reached the mouth of Caine's Creek. He stood on the pedals and forced himself to pedal uphill.

When he rounded the last curve before Van's house, he saw Van out in the yard bent down low under the hood of an old, rusted 80's model sports car. He didn't notice Blake coming. Blake jumped off his bike and let it roll to a crash in the ditch next to Van's yard. He scaled the tiny embankment that led up to where Van was standing. It all happened so fast. Before Van could look up, Blake grabbed the hood of the car and slammed it with as much force and anger as he could gather.

The hood slammed down on top of Van and he let out a lengthy strand of obscenities. Blake raised the hood and slammed it down again and again and then jumped on top of it.

"I know what you did," Blake said. "I know it was you! And you went too far!"

"You little shit!" Van screamed. "I don't know what you're talking about. I'm gonna kill you! Let me out of here!"

Blake jumped off the hood and pulled Van from underneath by his belt. He punched him in the bridge of the nose. He heard a loud pop and blood oozed from Van's nostrils. He staggered back and fell into the car. Blake hit him again. And again.

"You went too far!" Blake repeated, holding a fistful of Van's faded black T-shirt. He pressed him into the bumper of the car. "If you ever touch her again. If you ever even look at her again. I will kill you."

Blake's voice was low and gravelly.

"What in the hell are you talking about?" Van whimpered.

"You know what I'm talking about!" Blake screamed. "Don't you dare deny it!"

"What's goin' on out here?" called a deep, raspy voice.

Blake turned to see a man standing on the porch of Van's house. Van's father, he presumed. The man came down the steps and before Blake knew it, the man had thrown him to the ground. He kicked Blake in the ribs and shoved him against the side of the porch so hard the weathered banisters rattled and flakes of old paint drifted from the cracked wood. The man stank of sweat and alcohol. He kicked Blake repeatedly and knelt to punch him, holding Blake's head off the ground by his hair.

"You bratty fucker! You don't come on my property and start beatin' on my boy."

"He deserved it," Blake said fearlessly, but the words were barely words at all. He was gasping for air from the kick to his rib and sternum and his mouth was about half full of blood.

In such a helpless position, Blake could tell just how big this man was. He was at least six feet tall with broad shoulders and a thick gut hanging over the waist of his jeans. He held his hand to Blake's throat, forcing his weight down upon him.

"Now this really don't seem fair now does it?"

Blake knew that voice. It was Cass.

"A grown man beatin' up on a little boy. Any man that'd do somethin' like that ought to be ashamed of himself if you ask me."

Van's dad looked at Cass. "Who in the hell are you? Anyway, nobody asked you. Get on out of here. This ain't your business."

"I think it is," Cass said. Blake had never seen Cass like this, not even when his temper flared. There was a look in his eye that was unnerving. His lips pressed thin.

Van's dad started to reply, but it was too late. Cass was upon him. Cass hit him three times and slammed his head into the porch. He fell to the ground and lay still. Van looked on in terror. Cass picked up a hefty rock, nearly the size of his fist and raised it high over his head.

Blake screamed before he could stop it. "Cass! No!"

Cass looked back at him with narrow eyes, breathing heavy. He grunted once and dropped the rock next to Van's dad, who lay unconscious on the ground.

"Come on, Blake," Cass said. "Let's get outta here."

***

Cass walked Blake up the road to the Bradley house. He offered to carry him, but Blake wouldn't hear of it. His body ached terribly, but he felt a duty to make it on his own. The least Cass could do was carry his bike and Blake allowed it.

They barely spoke on the way. When they reached the house they went inside and sat at the kitchen table. Cass rummaged around the house looking for something to clean Blake's wounds. After searching the bathroom, he returned with a dusty bottle of rubbing alcohol and a washcloth.

"Boy, I gotta ask," Cass said. "What were you doing fighting those guys?"

"I had to," Blake said, and in spite of his efforts, a tear streamed down his face and formed a droplet at his chin, daring to fall. "I had to."

"Can't believe I'm about to say this, but violence ain't always the answer. Especially when them two cusses were a lot bigger than you. I will say you messed the boy up pretty good though." Cass gave him a playful slap in the shoulder.

"I didn't plan on fighting his dad. But Van had to pay. He hurt her. He did awful things to her. They hurt Greta, Cass!"

Cass's face went slack. His brow no longer furrowed and his lips no longer pursed. His mouth hung slightly open.

"Yeah, I guess he did need to pay then. Is she okay?"

"The doctors said she'll be fine. But it shouldn't have happened. He had no right to put his hands on her!"

Cass rubbed his chin. It sounded like sandpaper scraping paint from a wall.

"You really care about that little girl, don't ya?"

"Yes. I would do anything for her. She's the best friend I've ever had."

"She's lucky to have you. And you her. But you shouldn't have went after those guys like that. If I hadn't come along when I did, you could've got hurt bad. Or worse."

"I'm fine," Blake said. "But thanks."

"Don't thank me," Cass said. "Don't ever thank me."

"Why?" Blake asked, a little surprised.

"I've done things in my life that I ain't proud of. And it seems like if I help people, it's just a piece of payin' back what I took from 'em."

"What do you mean, Cass?" Blake asked, dabbing his scraped elbows with alcohol. "What have you done that's so bad?"

"Just don't thank me," he persisted.

"Fair enough," Blake said. "I won't."

***

Blake started home just before it got dark. It hurt to ride his bicycle, but if he walked it would take him forever to get there. He rode calmly, not even worrying that Van or his dad may be out and about. He just thought of Greta, and how this was one ride she couldn't make with him.

19

It was nearing midnight when Blake laid his bike down next to his dad's tool shed. He wasn't worried about what his parents were inevitably going to say. Thoughts of heroes ran through his head—and villains—and the thin curtain that blew in the wind between the two.

The house was mostly dark except for a faint lamp's glow and the flash of the TV in the living room. He could see Dianne on the couch with a book open in her lap, likely studying to the chatter of the television. He hated that they didn't talk much anymore. For a moment, he thought about going in there, but went up the stairs and to his room instead.

It was 11:37 according the clock on his nightstand. His body ached and his mind ran circles around the absurdity of it all. *Things like this happened on TV, in books. They weren't supposed to happen in real life.* He had found himself thinking that a lot lately. He thought of Greta laying in her hospital bed, her father no doubt wide awake at her bedside.

Blake threw himself onto his bed face first. The next time he was aware of anything he was waking up to the sun on his face through the open window, still in his dirty jeans and T-shirt, shoes still on his feet.

He took a bath and changed into clean clothes before going down to breakfast.

His parents weren't in the kitchen. He could see his mom outside on the porch sitting in the glider with a washtub of corn in front of her, no sign of his dad. She was bundled in a thick brown jacket. The clock on the kitchen wall explained it. It was 2 in the afternoon. He'd slept over half the day but he didn't feel rested. He felt more tired than he did before he went to sleep. And he only wanted one thing: to see Greta.

"I just let you sleep," Patty said when Blake stepped out onto the porch. "You looked out of it. Figured you wouldn't want to go to school anyway."

"You figured right," Blake said.

It didn't take much to convince her to let him ride to the hospital with Charlotte, who had taken the day off work. After a brief car ride, he was standing with her in front of the same elevator as yesterday, with just a slightly different frame of mind.

Greta was awake when he entered the room. Her eyes opened wider when she saw him.

"Blake! What happened to you?"

At first, he didn't even realize what she was talking about. For some reason he hadn't thought that the fight had taken a visual toll on him. He looked in the open bathroom door at the mirror above the sink and saw a dark circle around his left eye and bruises on the side of his neck. It shocked him slightly, but not as much as the fact that his mom didn't even mention it.

"I'm fine," he said.

"I didn't ask you how you were," Greta said sympathetically. "What happened?"

He sat down and said, "I had to get him for what he did to you."

"Are you ok?"

He smiled. "Like I said before, I'm fine. How are you?"

"My head still hurts a little. But that's not the worst. The doctors have been doing some weird tests. They say I'll be fine in time though."

"That's good."

"I have to ask. Who did you go after?"

His eyes widened. "Van, for what he did to you." He suddenly felt nervous.

"How do you know it was him?"

"How could it not be? Who else would do something like this?"

"I'm not sure. I'll tell you what I told the police. The man's voice was deep, but I didn't get a look at him. He seemed like a bigger guy though." She began to shake. "Van's voice is sort of high-pitched if I remember correctly. And he may be tall, but he's sort of scrawny in a way." She looked down to her fidgeting hands resting in her lap. "I don't think it was him."

Blake played the scene instantly over in his head, remembering Van's persistent reassurance that he had no idea what Blake was talking about when he mentioned what had happened to Greta. He remembered Van's voice. It *was* sort of high. He remember Van's dad, who had a much deeper voice. The voice had called to him from behind from the porch as he repeatedly ran his fist into Van's face. Then he remembered the beating from Van's dad until Cass had saved him.

***

Kenneth S. Harris

Days passed and Greta remained set on the road to recovery. Blake visited a couple more times, but by the end of the week her parents were talking of her coming home. It was cold. Autumn was aging and winter was an eager replacement. Vernon called Saturday night with the good news: Greta would be home before noon the next day.

Blake was so excited he couldn't sleep. He lay awake all night longing for things to get back to normal, for he and Greta to resume their friendship from somewhere other than bedside at a hospital. Of course, he would do it all over again, and to greater extremes if need be. If he had his way, he would have stayed by her bedside every day and into the night, fell asleep holding her hand sitting in the lousy waiting room chair he had pulled up close to her bed, his head on the sheets that stank of sterility, yet somehow smelled familiar and pleasant with the aroma of his best friend.

But truth be told, if he could have had his way, none of this would have ever happened. He would have woken up earlier on the morning it had happened. He would have been on time. No, he would have been early. And Greta would have been fine.

Restless at a little after 1 a.m., Blake decided to step outside for some air. Sleep wasn't coming. He crept out his window and onto the overhang of the house as he'd done so many times before. He was shaking. It may have been from the cold, but he thought anticipation for the next day had something to do with it as well. For a while he just sat on the overhang and watched the sky, clear and calm, plenty of stars. A chilled breeze was blowing and he had to hug himself tightly to stay somewhat warm.

He decided to climb down the overhang and drop onto the ground. He felt like walking. It almost seemed like he was sleepwalking. Nothing quite seemed real. He saw the single sheet of paper tacked to the tree before he had taken two steps. Shocked, he ran to the tree and pulled the note free. He unfolded it and read the lanky scrawled handwriting, knowing it was from Cass.

Boy, I'm sorry about what happened to your friend. Send her my best.
- Cass

Blake folded the paper into a tiny ball and up the side of the porch he went, onto the overhang and back through his window. He was feeling considerably better, hearing from Cass and all. He crawled back in bed, head full of thoughts.

It was nearing 3 a.m. when he finally drifted off to sleep, uninterrupted by dreams, waking instantly as though something had erased six hours of his life. He ignored the dull ache in his bones when he got out of bed, mere remnants of the pain he had experienced less than a week ago. He dressed quickly and ran downstairs and to the front door, gazing across the field to Greta's house. Her parents' car wasn't in the driveway. He returned to the kitchen for breakfast.

His family wasn't home. They had probably gone to church knowing it was useless to try to coax Blake into going this particular Sunday, with Greta coming home and all. He poured himself a bowl of cereal and sat alone eating it much faster than he normally would, clearly and senselessly telling himself that the faster breakfast ended, the sooner Greta would be home.

The phone rang when there were still a few spoonfuls to go. He ran to the receiver and jerked it from its cradle.

"Hello."

"Where are you?" Greta said. "I haven't seen you in days. And with me coming home today, I figured you would be sitting on my front porch waiting."

"Are you home?" Blake asked. His pulse was racing.

"I am! You should come over right now. I've missed you, you know?"

Without another word, Blake slammed the receiver down and bolted out the doorway and down the steps. He ran straight through the corn field, littered with shucks, clearly overtaken by cold weather. Greta stepped out the front door when he was merely a few feet from the bottom of the steps and he swore he had never seen her look prettier. She was wearing a red blouse, a purple fleece coat and blue jeans. Yes, she was beautiful, more so than ever and for reasons he couldn't even begin to understand.

He ran up the steps and to her side. He hugged her gently in spite of every impulse yelling for him to squeeze her tight and lift her off the ground.

"I'm so glad you're okay," he said.

"Me too. Things will be back to normal in no time."

He thought of normal, and of Van. He were part of the normal routine that led to tragedy. So perhaps normal needed to change.

In truth, he had been thinking far too much about who had committed the crime. Van had paid for it already, regardless of the culprit, but Blake still wondered if he had done the right thing.

He considered asking her again, "Are you sure it wasn't Van?" but thought better of it. He didn't want this day tainted in any way. He kissed her cheek and they walked inside the house where her parents greeted them warmly and insisted Blake stay for dinner.

Even with her parents' on-looking eyes, they held hands tightly. He was determined that today would be the first day of their new normal.

***

It was Wednesday before Greta returned to school. Her parents thought it best if she took a couple more days to recuperate at home. When she boarded the bus with Blake Wednesday morning, some people stared, some looked down at their laps, and others looked intently out the windows. Word about what happened to her had somehow gotten around, it seemed.

They sat in their normal seat and tried to ignore the growing tension on the bus. On a typical morning, a buzz of hushed chatter filled the air, including Blake and Greta's morning chit chat. But this particular morning, there was only an uncomfortable silence.

Blake and Greta experienced an array of reaction to their presence throughout the day, ranging from awkward cold shoulders and fleeting glances to an occasional, nervous "hello" or "I'm so sorry."

Blake also learned that word had spread about his confrontation with Van. In the eyes of the afterschool victim, Blake was a hero. He paid it no mind, just stayed at Greta's side whenever possible.

The day trudged on sluggishly, but the final bell sounded at last. Blake left his final class a few minutes early and walked to the sixth grade buildings to meet Greta outside her classroom. He walked her to the bus, and settling into his seat next to her. As the school bus carried them home, he caught a glimpse of Van outside Bachman's Pawn getting into a vehicle with some other boys. He was wearing large black sunglasses but the bruises on his face could still be seen around the lenses. Blake took some satisfaction in the fact that he looked like hell.

Blake had also heard throughout the day that Van had been questioned by the police. He wondered what had come of that. He tried to imagine Van falling to his knees and helplessly confessing everything he had done to Greta to the cops.

***

Blake and Greta took some time off from playing outdoors, distancing themselves from Caine's Creek, even if it meant seeing less of Cass. They spent evening after evening indoors drawing, watching TV and such. Blake taught Greta to whittle small figurines out of pieces of wood; she taught him to play a few tunes on the piano, though he had a few problems getting his left and right hands to cooperate at the same time.

By the time the first flurries arrived, they decided it was time to head back outdoors. Luckily, both of their parents agreed that enough time had passed, but still wanted them not to wander.

On a chilly Friday evening free of snow, the two rode their bikes down to the mouth Crystal Creek and sat on the bank skipping stones across the gentle ripples of the water. They were both bundled in heavy jackets: Greta's a loud shade of purple with a yellow lining; Blake's a casual and faded brown.

Blake finally decided it was time. If he didn't say something soon it was going to eat him up inside.

"Can I ask you something?" he said without looks at her, but keeping his eyes on the water as a stone skipped across. "I mean, it's okay if you don't want me to. I just thought I would ask and see."

"Blake, you can ask me anything." She smiled and held his hand.

He looked at her and, oddly enough, noticed her lips were chapped. And in her bright clothes, with her blue eyes, she contrasted the gray sky of winter like a rainbow that showed up too soon.

"If it wasn't Van. Who do you think it was?" As he spoke, he could hardly stand to look in her eyes.

"I don't know," she said. "But Van is just a boy, even though he's bigger than us. His voice, his hands and arms. The person who attacked me had a deep voice and big round arms. It wasn't a boy. Not even one Van's size."

Blake's mind began to race immediately. He didn't dare say anything he was thinking out loud. He just drew her close to him in a gentle hug. He didn't want to, but he found himself treating her like she was so fragile, as if she would break if he let slip only for a moment the utmost

Kenneth S. Harris

care. He hated that he saw her that way, and even tried not to. For now, at least, Greta was a girl made of glass.

20

Winter set in with full force and ripped into Hemingford with a gale of icy weather. Greta's bruises faded away to nothing and school became redundantly bland. Blake could tell it was getting close to Christmas, because Dianne's Christmas spirit was bubbling over and seeping into every crevice of the Kiser residence. She had insisted the family begin decorating almost immediately after Thanksgiving, and hung colorful wreaths, draped garland along the banisters to the front porch, and put the traditional centerpiece on the kitchen table—an assortment of plastic flowers surrounded by holly and sprigs of mistletoe—all of which had been tucked away neatly into the otherwise neglected attic of the Kiser home.

Blake had no trouble deciding what he would get Greta for Christmas. He'd seen in it in a department store weeks ago on a trip to town with his mother. It was a tiny trinket, likely meant to be hung from a necklace. But Blake had other intentions for it. He was going to buy Greta a pack of shoestrings—bright blue to match her loud personality—and attach the trinket to the strings. It seemed like the sort of offbeat fashion Greta would appreciate. And for some reason when he looked at Greta, he couldn't help but think of shoes.

The trinket was a tiny house, squared with an A-frame roof. Blake liked it because when suspended in mid-air as such, dangling about at the end of a chain, it reminded him of the farmhouse that landed in Oz, taking Dorothy from a mundane existence on a farm, where every day was close to a copy of the day before, to a land of excitement, adventure, and oddities otherwise unseen to the ordinary eye. While it's true Greta had loved the book, *The Wizard of Oz*, truly, she had also been his vessel out of the mundane.

For a personal touch, he decided he would also carve something as well, something small to replace her necklace. That would give him something to do at night to pass the time until Christmas.

The first considerable snow fell during the first week of December, after many frost-laden nights that felt like winter's zenith to the adjusting world. Blake lay in his bed looking out his window and up at the night sky, the silhouettes of trees accentuated by the lone pole light on the Kiser farm. It was the light that showed Blake the first flakes of the season. When he looked just beneath the light, as he had been taught throughout childhood, a fine mist of drifting snow danced there, drifting down into the darkness below. Before long the mist became a swirl of thick snow that quickly coated the ground, power lines, and tree branches. Blake watched for hours before drifting to sleep.

The snow added up to about eight inches and stuck around for days, giving Blake and Greta the chance to play in it. They built snowmen, rode sleds down the hill behind Greta's house, and threw an unwavering supply of snowballs. Blake found it so odd to lie in his bed and gaze out the window at Greta's house and not see towering corn stalks between them. The field was flat now; the giant stalks nothing but a memory that would return after hours of hard labor the following summer.

Greta couldn't believe that school had been canceled over eight inches of snow. "We used to get ten or twelve inches in Greenwich and school never got canceled. You all just don't know how to drive down here," she said, giggling.

By the time the weather had cleared up enough for them to return to school, there was only one week left before the start of Christmas vacation. Blake panicked! He had been spending so much time with Greta, he'd forgotten to get things in order for her Christmas present. He rode into town one afternoon with his mother and picked up the shoe strings and the trinket, which took all the money he had saved. That night he cut a chunk from a branch of the tree that stood at the corner of the back porch and began whittling, unsure what he would create at first.

As he chipped away the bark of the branch and began cutting into the flesh of the wood, it became clear: he would carve her a grand oak tree—a giant she could hold in the palm of her hand, just like the one out back from which he had cut the branch, just like the one with the tire swing she had loved so much that stood behind Cass's house. He could see it now, dangling from a chain around her neck.

Blake worked for hours, losing track of time completely. It wasn't until the sun peaked in his bedroom window the next morning that he realized he had, for the first time in his life, stayed awake an entire night.

The tree was about an inch and a half tall. He worked the last bit of detail into it and left a place to adhere it to the chain. He laid it on the table and took a step back to appreciate his work. *Greta will love it!* he thought with pride. It truly was the perfect tree.

***

Blake placed Greta's collected Christmas gifts in the top drawer of his dresser before school. They would be safe there: safe from Greta finding them, safe from Diana stumbling across them and mistaking them as a gift for her.

School was most unwelcome in the coming days. It caused time to creep by slowly, while all Blake could think about was the upcoming holiday and giving Greta her gift. He could imagine her face when she saw it, often closing his eyes in class and playing the scene out in his head, her eyes wide, her cheeks aglow, and her beautiful, precious lips all smiles.

The halls seemed lonely. He wished Greta were in seventh grade. He found himself going to class all alone, only the spirit of his friend in tow. He remembered the sixth-grade buildings well. They made winters more difficult to bear. Going from class to class was hindered by the bite of an icy breeze or the occasional snow flurry. Remembering himself doing so, he pictured Greta scurrying across the wooden walkway with a mess of books in hand. She never talked of any, but he was sure she had made many friends in her own grade, and he pictured them, odd and faceless, scampering at her sides.

At last, the final day arrived. The last day of school before Christmas! Excitedly, Blake and Greta met at their usual spot in between their houses to wait for the bus. Blake showed up 10 minutes early, as was his routine since the unspeakable incident that befell Greta. He didn't know it then, but perhaps, he would never be late again in his life as a result of that day.

They boarded the bus in silence, both still shaking off the drowsiness of the early morning. Greta spoke first.

"Wait 'til you see what I got you for Christmas," she said proudly.

Blake's forehead had been pressed against the glass of the bus window, chilly on his skin as he watched the grass, trees and houses pass them by.

"I don't want to guess," he said. "I'd rather just wait and find out."

"Well, that's no fun!" Greta teased. "You're supposed to inquire!"

"I'm supposed to 'inquire?'" he laughed. "You and your big words."

"'Inquire' isn't a big word," she laughed.

"It's bigger than 'ask.' Anyway, I can't wait to give you your present. I worked really hard on it."

"So, I take it that it's something you made?" she smirked.

"Wait... I mean... I didn't mean..."

She laughed and laid her head on his shoulder. "I'm sorry. No more tricks."

The day seemed to creep by, each tick of a clock's second hand seeming heavy and regretful. He sat lifeless in each class listening to the teachers and pretending to

Kenneth S. Harris

care, when his mind was streaked with nothing but scenes of anticipation of the days to come.

Blake saw someone he did not expect as he exited the warmth of the main building and headed across the parking lot for art class, thankfully the last class of the day. His unexpected visitor wore faded jeans, ripped at the knees, an old leather jacket and fine, fuzzy hair on his chin. He leaned against the chain-link fence smoking a cigarette, allowing his exhales to mix smoke with his visible breath as he sucked it back into his nostrils like an evil dragon, lurking, waiting, watching.

Van motioned for Blake to come. Blake stood frozen, yet ignoring the chill of the day. His chill had come from inside the moment he laid eyes on Van. *What is he doing here?* Blake thought. *He's supposed to be in alternative school.*

He motioned for Blake to come again, and this time Blake glanced about and at last took a few steps towards him. Van disappeared behind the art building and Blake found himself anxious to follow, his fists clenched in rage. If Van wanted to show up here, he would give him a few good reasons to never do so again.

Blake stepped around the side of the building and saw Van stamping out his cigarette in a thin layer of filthy snow.

"What are you doing here?" Blake demanded, not even bothering to monitor the volume of his voice.

"Easy, man," Van said. "I ain't here to start nothing."

"Then why *are* you here?"

"I heard what happened to your little girlfriend," Van said.

"Her name is Greta," Blake said coldly.

"Ok, Greta! Chill out, man. I just wanted to say that I'm sorry as hell for what happened."

Blake was awestruck. He started to speak but—

"I also heard you thought it was me that did it. I take it that's why you jumped me that day?"

"Don't even play around. I know it was you!"

"Like hell it was! Me and my buddies like to mess around with you kids. We might push you down in the mud, even black an eye or two, but we would never go that far!"

Blake thought hard about this. Van seemed sincere, which was something Blake had never heard from the boy before.

"And I reckon I owe you a good thumpin' after what you and your pal put me and my old man through. But you know? I figure you've been through enough shit. So you get a free pass. This time."

Van walked past him and nudged him into the building.

"But I really am sorry. By the way, who was your pal?"

"That was Cass," Blake said. "You should know him. He lives right up the road from you."

"Never seen him before," Van said. "He's a mean old cuss though. Anyway, I hope Greta is feeling okay."

And as quickly as he had shown up, Van was gone. Blake stood there, uncharacteristically late for class, yet tardiness never entered his brain. He was still discovering ways of coping with what had happened to Greta, but hating Van had always been his fail-safe. When all else ended in sadness, he could rely on hating Van to pull him through. Now this! This show of emotion had caught him off guard, left him wondering how the same guy he had just spoken with could be capable of an act so heinous.

For the first time in his life, Blake skipped his last class that day and stood in the cold thinking. Before the bell rang, he slipped around the side of the building and onto the walkway that led to the sixth-grade buildings. He met Greta just outside her last class and they caught the bus together. On the surface, Blake couldn't stop smiling, yet inside his thoughts churned just like his stomach.

21

Blake forced all thoughts of Van and his claim to innocence from his mind. Too many good things were just around the corner for him to be dwelling on the bad. School was out for Christmas break; Jenna would be arriving tomorrow, and staying with him and his family throughout the holidays; and before long, Blake could bestow Greta with her gift on which he had worked so hard.

Blake doubled up on covers that night, as he often did in the winter. The house only had one pot-bellied stove downstairs, which seldom heated his room. They had a space heater, but he was glad to let Dianne keep it in her room at night.

He stared out the window for some time. The night-time sky was coal black with hardly any visible stars. A wisp of cloud framed the growing moon.

Blake remembered what Christmas used to be like, and how different it would be this year. Past Christmases had begun on Christmas Eve with Jenna showing up around 4:30 in the afternoon for their first get together. Arthur and Dory would accompany her but only because Aunt Dory wanted them to join as a family. Arthur kept a permanent beer in his hand throughout the festivities and displayed his disapproval for being there with the occasional belch or mumble under his breath. Yet Blake could still see Jenna's smiling face as the two of them ripped into their gifts. This year would contain no un-pleasantries from Uncle Arthur, but it would likely contain much fewer smiles from Jenna.

His thoughts delivered him into a dreamless sleep with covers stacked snug against his chin. He woke the next morning still freezing. He sat up and got dressed quickly. He rushed through a quick bath, and even through breakfast. He retrieved the trinkets from his room and tucked them into his jeans pocket. He ran outside, down the steps, and towards Greta's house. *So strange*, he thought, *I can now cut through the corn field without minding the rows.* None was left standing in the frosty chill of the winter season.

"Stay close by," Elden shouted, but Blake was barely cognizant of the phrase.

He rang the doorbell and stood impatiently waiting for someone to answer. It was Greta who opened the heavy front door.

"Great minds think alike, I see," she said, noticing they were both bundled up and ready to brave the cold morning.

***

"I wish there was more snow," Blake said, as they sat idly in the barn loft.

"Yeah, I miss it. We never had many cool places to sled in the city."

"Just you wait. When the next snow hits, we'll sled all day. You'll be sick of sledding by the time we're through," he laughed.

Blake thumbed the tiny trinkets in his pocket, toying with the idea of not waiting for Christmas to arrive. The anticipation was killing him. He wanted nothing more than to fish them out and give them to her now, but he was afraid it would ruin the holiday.

"Looks like we have company," Greta said, sitting up from where she was laying on a thick bale of hay.

Jenna's Corolla was approaching slowly down the tiny dirt road that led to Blake's driveway. The only car on the road, it looked lonely with a small puff of dust trailing the tires, moving persistently amidst a backdrop of still, gray morning.

"I hope she's okay," Blake said. "I haven't talked to her much since, well, you know."

"Let's go," Greta said.

The two of them clambered down the ladder that connected the floor to the barn loft and bolted out the large double doors of the barn. They reached the end of the driveway and were waiting when Jenna pulled in. She smiled when she saw them and peered at them with thankful eyes over her dark sunglasses, which she wore despite the scarceness of the sun on that particular morning.

"Merry Christmas, you two!" she said, getting out of the tiny car and hugging them both.

Blake noticed the backseat was filled with presents, and it settled on him that he had completely forgotten to get something for Jenna. They typically didn't exchange much. Perhaps a drawing or a small wooden figure. But Blake had been so excited about Greta's gift that he had completely forgotten his dear cousin. Two days to go was definitely not enough time to carve anything worthy of what may rest in the mountainous packages in the back-seat.

His heart sank that much more when he heard her say, "Blake, care to give me a hand with these?" as she opened the trunk to reveal another pile of colorfully-wrapped gifts.

***

Blake considered his options: ask his parents for some extra money to buy a last-minute gift for Jenna, but he knew better; he couldn't save his lunch money because there was no more school before Christmas; he could carve something, but felt it wouldn't be worthy of whatever rested inside the large boxes he had helped drag out of Jenna's trunk. He decided to turn to the only other grownup he knew that may be able to help—-Cass.

He and Greta planned to leave early the next morning after telling their parents they were only going a short way on their bikes. But neither of their parents would hear of it, especially when the police had made zero progress in figuring out who had attacked Greta, as well as zero progress in discovering who had murdered Jenna's parents.

Blake came clean and confessed that he and Greta wanted to see Cass since it was Christmas. "You remember?" Blake said. "They guy who saved our lives?" It had no effect on his parents, but Jenna was another story. She offered to take them, but Blake was reluctant at first, since it was her gift he would be discussing with Cass. After weighing his options though, he decided to take her up on it.

"Where exactly do you want to go? Who do you want to visit?" she asked as she and Blake sat up late in his room drawing pictures and talking about years passed.

"To the head of Caine's Creek. The man we saw at..." his voice trailed off and his cheeks flushed. "He lives all alone and we want to take him a present and wish him a Merry Christmas."

"Sounds fine to me."

"Cool. So, we'll leave around nine in the morning?"

"Actually," she said, "let's leave a little after noon. It doesn't take as long to get to Caine's Creek when you have four wheels instead of two."

22

Jenna was right. Instead of the hour and a half the trip took on a bike, they reached their destination in a little under 20 minutes.

"You mean to tell me he lives *here?*" Jenna said, her eyes wide with disbelief.

"Yeah, he's been trying to fix up the place," Blake said with a shaky voice.

Jenna said nothing and twisted her lips in confusion. "Blake Kiser, are you trying to trick me? No one lives here."

"No! I swear!"

"Well, I can see why your dad didn't want you visiting him in this place," she replied.

"Please give him a chance, Jenna," Greta said from the backseat. "He's actually a really nice man."

"Okay," she said. "I just hope the inside of the house is nicer than the outside."

As Jenna got out of the car, Blake leaned to Greta and whispered, "Try to keep her busy while I talk to Cass about her gift."

He hoped Cass would have something nice lying around that a girl would appreciate. He also hoped Cass would let him do chores for it, or trade him something. Perhaps, but not likely, Cass may loan him some money to buy Jenna a gift.

They got out of the car and walked the familiar cobbled stone walkway—familiar to Blake and Greta, but completely odd to Jenna, who seemed to walk on her tiptoes. The grass had yet to be cut, and had died at full height in the winter's frost. Blake knocked three solid times. After a moment's silence, they heard heavy footfalls opposite the door and within seconds Cass threw it back.

He looked grizzled, with a thick beard and dirty face. His clothes were tattered and stained, and his eyes were wide with surprise. But before Blake could offer a friendly hello, he wondered why Cass had opened the front door. He always wanted them to come around back. It hadn't occurred to him while he had walked the steps and knocked, not even while standing on the front porch. But seeing the anger—yes, wild anger—in Cass's eyes, it hit him like a sack full of rocks.

"Get in here, now!" Cass shouted, and pulled them inside.

Jenna started to speak in terrified protest once the heavy door slammed shut behind them, but Cass cut her off.

"Boy, we have to talk. Alone." He crossed the living room in a hurry and motioned Blake into the kitchen. Jenna stood frozen with fear, while Greta eyed Blake nervously.

Blake nodded, assuring her it was okay, and followed Cass.

"Why did you bring *her* here?" Cass barked as soon as they were out of sight, pointing towards the living room.

"She's my cousin. Remember, you met her at the cemetery?"

Cass grabbed two handfuls of his messy, black hair and pulled.

"I don't need a bunch of people knowing I'm staying here! You knew that!"

Blake didn't know what to say. He stammered and stood frozen somewhere between guilt for betraying his friend, and fear of Cass's unexpected hostility.

"Cass, I'm-I'm sorry," he stammered. "I didn't think it would be a big deal."

"Well, it is a big deal!" Cass hissed.

Blake backed into a wobbly, old table with piles of clothes stacked on top. The smell of mildew and misuse erupted from the pile.

"Why don't you want anybody to know you're staying here?"

"Because, this is *not* my house! You know that! You *should* know that! You may be a kid, but you're not that dumb. I'm just using it to keep the wind and rain off my back for a while, and a lot of folks wouldn't appreciate it. Even though, nobody's using it right now. You understand? Too many people find out, I'll be out in the hills again, fightin' off the weather and wild animals. Hell, I'll probably be dead in a week or two."

"Cass, calm down. I'm sorry," Blake urged quietly. "Jenna is my family. I've known her since I was a baby. You can trust her."

"I don't trust nobody," Cass said.

"That's not true," said Blake. "You trust me. And you trust Greta. Or else you would have never have been our friend."

Cass's eyes filled with sadness. His eyelids filled quickly and tears streaked his filthy cheeks.

"Blake!" Jenna screamed from the other room. "We have to go! We have to go now!"

Blake couldn't force his mind from Cass. But after a few moments' silence, Jenna came into the room and grabbed his arm and began tugging him towards the door. Her eyes were red, wet, and wide with terror. She was holding a dirty, patchwork quilt under her arm.

"Jenna, let go!" Blake said, resisting being pulled from his friend's side. "I can't leave yet."

"Blake, please!" she cried.

"Hey, what do you got there?" Cass roared. "Give me that back! You tryin' to steal from me?"

"We have to go now!" she screamed at the top of her lungs. But it was too late. Cass grabbed Jenna's arm in one hand and the quilt in the other. He tugged at her ferociously. The quilt tore with an unsettling rasp.

Jenna fell to the ground, accidentally pulling Blake along with her. And Cass was upon them, tearing at the quilt and anything else that got in his way. But Jenna refused to let go. Her screams filled the air and made it thick, difficult to breathe. Blake noticed a ravenous gleam in Cass's eyes—the same penetrating glare he had noticed when Cass had held the rock above Van's dad with every intention of smashing it into the man's skull. He kicked at Cass with all of his might, and clung to Jenna, who was scared stiff, taking in quick, panicked gasps of air.

The sound of breaking glass mingled with Jenna's screams, Blake's gasps, and Cass's raving growls. Shards sprinkled Blake and Jenna as Cass stumbled to the side.

Greta stood above him, her face twisted into a terrified grimace and tears poured down her face in waves. For a moment, all was silent apart from Greta's hysterical cries.

Cass fell to his hands and knees and shook his head back and forth and blinked his eyes hard. Blood matted his hair and dripped onto the floor.

"Run!" Jenna screamed. She grabbed at Blake and Greta and ran for the door, both children stumbling as she pushed them along.

"Come back here!' Cass roared. "I'm sorry. I... I..." Cass sucked at much-needed air. "I didn't mean to hurt you..." But his voice trailed off, and the details of his speech went mostly unnoticed. The three of them got into Jenna's car quickly—slamming doors echoed against the lonely hillside.

Jenna screamed again when she saw him stumble out the front door. She backed out and turned the car in a muddy wide spot still wet from the day's momentary thaw. For a moment, the wheels only spun in the filthy muck, but eventually the tiny car crawled its way out and sped down the road much too fast for the tiny one-lane.

No one spoke until they were at the mouth of Caine's Creek, ready to turn onto the main road which would eventually lead them home. Blake held Greta the whole way while they both silently sobbed to pounding heart-beats. In their panic, they had both ended up in the front seat.

As Jenna turned onto the main two-lane road, it wasn't long until panicked sobs overtook her. She pulled onto the shoulder and wailed with her head against the steering wheel.

Kenneth S. Harris

"What happened back there?" Blake asked as his tears began to yield enough so that he could talk. "Why... What's up with this?" he asked, taking hold of the quilt, which was sprawled in tattered drapes across Jenna's lap.

"Blake this isn't his quilt," she sobbed, trying to quell her own outburst. "This quilt belonged to my mother."

23

"Jenna, how can you be sure?" Blake asked in defiance. He folded his arms across his chest and glared at her in disbelief.

"This is how," Jenna said, pointing to the pattern of what was left of the quilt.

Blake, Greta, and Jenna had been in Blake's room since they had gotten back to the house. They were trying to calm down and approach what had happened with a clear head. Luckily, in Blake's eyes, his parents and Dianne were not home when they returned.

The pattern Jenna was pointing to was very specific and colorful, a patchwork of solid colors, designs, and patterns held together by a strong red stitching.

"I know this quilt!" Jenna shouted. "My mother made this quilt. We've had it since I was a little girl. I'm surprised you haven't seen it before."

"It's just... Cass has always been such a good friend," Blake said.

"He didn't look like a very good friend today," Jenna said matter-of-factly, wrapping the tattered quilt around her shoulders as she shivered.

"I don't know why..."

"Blake! Wake up! The man is bad news! He doesn't live there! He's squatting in a house that doesn't belong to him. He tried to hurt us today, maybe even kill us. And more importantly..." Her shout shrank, became a meek tremble on her lips. "I think he killed my parents."

"That's insane!" Blake screamed. "Cass wouldn't do anything like that! How can you even say it?"

"Well, why does he have their quilt in his shack?"

They glared at each other, their noses only inches from touching.

"Please, calm down," Greta said. "Both of you."

She sat on Blake's bed with her arms wrapped around her knees. She'd barely made a peep since they had gotten back to the house.

"Let's try to think about this logically," she said.

Jenna's eyes grew wide. "Well, aren't you the mature one?"

"I try," Greta said, sarcastically. "Now, seriously. Let's think about this. Blake, I understand why you are angry with Jenna for accusing Cass of something so terrible. But let's face it, she has a couple of good points. But please, no more yelling. I can't stand it.

"Jenna, think about it. There are other ways Cass could have gotten your parents' quilt. The house has been empty for a long time now. Maybe he broke in, completely by chance, and stole it. That's not good, of course. But it's a long way from murder. Have you been back to your house since you go there?"

"Well, no. I—"

"And who knows, maybe there's a small chance that you're mistaken. Maybe it's not the same quilt at all. We all make mistakes, especially when we're this upset.

"And Blake, I know you think Cass is a great man. And I'm not arguing with you there. He's helped us out of more binds than I care to remember. But did you see the way he was acting today? I was scared to death!" Her voice quivered. "So, try to understand why Jenna would think he's so crazy, and perhaps even dangerous. I'm afraid for now we're just going to have to settle on 'we don't know.'"

Jenna and Blake both stared at Greta with mouths hanging open. Silence surrounded them.

"You plan on being a lawyer, right?" Jenna said. "Because with a mouth like that, you better be."

***

Greta stayed at Blake's house until his parents got home, which was well after dark. They had been doing last-minute Christmas shopping, and had brought Dianne along with them. Blake and Jenna both walked Greta home, walking briskly on the way there and on the way back, considering Cass knew where Blake lived.

Tomorrow was Christmas Eve, Blake remembered. Somehow, it had slipped his mind. He turned the trinkets over and over in his pockets. He took them out and placed them back in his top dresser drawer before changing into his pajamas. He peered into the guest room before turning in and saw Jenna sleeping with the tattered bits of the quilt snuggled tightly against her face. Her bare feet protruded from the blanket that was covering her, so he tiptoed inside and pulled it down to cover them. His mother had always told him, "you catch a cold in your feet and in your chest. Keep 'em warm!"

He knew Cass would reach out to him soon and explain everything. There had to be an explanation, he knew it. He turned out the lamp by his bedside and blew a vaporous kiss in the direction of Greta's house before lying down. He expected racing thoughts and conflict to crowd his brain, make it impossible to sleep, but he was asleep as soon as his cheek hit the icy pillow.

***

When Blake woke up it was still dark outside, not even a hint of daylight. He sat up and squinted and peered out the window, vaguely aware of some dream he may have been having. Despite layers of sheets and blankets, he was frozen to the bone.

He put his feet on the floor, but quickly recoiled at the bite of the icy floorboards. He slipped on socks and his sneakers then tried again. He took extra soft steps to quiet the thud of his shoes on the wooden floor as he stepped out into the hall and descended the steps. No one else seemed to be awake.

The clock in the kitchen ticked a staccato rhythm throughout the house. It was ten minutes 'til six. Blake walked to the fridge and took out the jug of milk and poured a couple of swallows into a glass from the cupboard, sniffing it before drinking to make sure it hadn't spoiled. His breath came out in puffs in the harsh light from the open refrigerator. He could see the Christmas tree in the living room from where he stood. It bore no lights, and the tinsel couldn't sparkle in the darkness of the early morning. The tree looked cold and dead, or at least dying.

He thought about waking Jenna or Dianne, just for company, but decided against it. He wasn't as scared as Jenna, so he decided to fetch part of Greta's gifts—the shoe strings and maybe the trinket—and deliver them to her front porch where she would find them as soon as she woke up and stepped outside. He would save the necklace for last, to give to her in person.

Jenna feared running into Cass outside, especially after dark, but Blake longed for it. He knew if he came upon his friend, they would talk and Cass would explain and everything would be okay. He tiptoed back upstairs as fast as he could and retrieved the shoestrings and the tiny house, placed them in a cigar box and wrapped it in blue paper, adorned with smiling snowmen. He did the same with the hand-carved tree after threading it with the last old chain he could find in the house. He placed a red bow on both, put on his coat, and headed quietly out the door.

By this time it was close to 6:30. The sun wasn't quite out yet, but it was significantly lighter. The sky was a dark gray and Blake thought he could still see stars. He cut through the empty corn field, walking at a steady pace. The ground was stiff with frost and crunched beneath his footfalls.

No one seemed to be awake in Greta's house either. All the lights were off, save for the porch light which they'd left on every night that Blake could remember since they moved in. He took care to be extra quiet as he climbed the steps and placed the box containing the shoestrings on the front banister. He set a rock on top of it in case a strong wind came along.

When he returned to his front porch, he stopped and stood perfectly still. The kitchen light was on and he saw someone moving about through the window. It was likely his mother, fully awake and starting a hefty breakfast fit for a holiday. Rather than explain himself, he slipped around the side of the house to climb up to his room, hoping the whole time he'd left the window unlocked.

He started his climb as quickly as possible, but reflexively cast a glance towards the tree that stood at the corner of the house. A white clump protruded from the tree, folded back under a piece of raised bark. Blake ran to the tree knowing it was a note from Cass.

He took the paper out and read carefully. It was a difficult task, as Cass's handwriting had never been great, and the paper had been wadded into a tight ball and stuffed beneath the bark. It had suffered hundreds of creases and was even a little soggy in the cold morning air.

His hands shook, but Blake read intently:

Boy,
When you're little you get to make choices. You get to be a good guy, or you get to be a bad guy. And sometimes you can't change it. You're making good choices so far boy. I made some bad ones. Somewhere down the line I stopped being a good guy. I don't even know how I did it. And I don't know how to stop.
I just want you to know it was me. All the bad shit you've been through. It was me. And I'm sorry. I never meant for nobody to get hurt. Sometimes the devil in the back of my brain comes out and I can't tell him no.
Don't you dare forgive me. I don't deserve it. Only one thing I deserve I reckon.

The Perfect Tree

Tell your cousin I'm sorry about her parents. If it makes it any better, I didn't mean to kill them. I was just hungry and they was in the wrong place at the wrong time. It was an accident.
And tell your little girlfriend I'm sorry and that I'll miss her.
And keep being a good guy.
- Cass

Blake wadded the paper in his hand and tears streamed down his face. He wanted to scream, but all he could do was suck the cold morning air into his lungs and feel its sting. He felt around in his pockets, locating his pocket knife. Sharp enough to whittle the finest detail into a hunk of oak, sharp enough to confront Cass and see that he pays for the evils he'd delivered into this world.

Blake got on his bike and rode as fast as he could for the old tattered house in the head of Caine's Creek.

***

There are a lot of things a tree is good for. In its life, you can hang a tire from it for recreation, climb it to a tall tree house, steal away bits to carve wonderful art—and in this regard it brings joy. In its death, cut it down and burn it, use it for warmth and cooking, or use it to build a house or a barn—and it provides sustenance. But there is a darker side to the ancients that stand for hundreds of years next to man's mere decades.

Blake stormed into Cass's house without knocking. The door was slightly open, but Blake shouldered it open anyway with all his might and went sprawling into the living room.

"Cass!" All his hatred boiled to the surface, as he had spent the bike ride thinking of Cass's hands selfishly tearing at Greta's clothes and running the course of her body. *She'd just a kid!* he thought. He was sick and blind with fury.

He thought about Jenna's pain, and his own, at never seeing his aunt or uncle again. Blake loved Aunt Dory as he did his own mother. And Arthur, despite his demons, didn't deserve death. Cass was right about himself. You can be a hero, or you can be a villain. The only difference can be as simple as a single choice.

"Cass! Where are you?" Blake screamed as he rummaged the house looking for the fiend he used to call a friend. Perhaps, he had already moved on since confessing.

Blake burst out the back door panting and raving, brandishing his knife tightly in his hand, the blade locked open and gleaming in the morning sun. But he was not prepared for what he saw. Cass's body swung from the end of a rope secured to a branch of the old oak tree. Beneath his feet, which hovered lifeless a mere two feet from the frozen grass, lay an overturned wooden chair and the old rotted tire swing that Greta had broken so many months ago.

Blake recoiled, falling back against the stoop of the house. He dropped his knife and cried alone in the backyard that truly belonged to no one.

24

Blake's legs suddenly had no bones in them, but he ran wobbling from side to side and gasping precious air. He fell down the stone steps at the front of the old yard and his body thumped the worm-eaten gate open with a dry scrape of the frosty ground. He picked up his bike and rode to the first home he came to, slung it to the ground and rushed the door with waning will to move. The little trailer belonged to Van's family.

He cried and thrashed and beat at the door until someone answered.

"Boy, what in the hell?" Van's father roared. "Get off my property. Now!"

Blake spoke in tormented cries. "Please help. Call my dad! Call the police! Call anybody!"

The man's face turned from fury to worry and his brow dropped down over his eyes and he squinted.

"Who is it, Dad?" Van called from inside the trailer.

"It's that little boy that kicked your ass," the man said, but the words were thick with worry. "He's cuttin' a fit. Boy, what are you goin' on about?"

"He's dead!" Blake screamed. "He's dead!" And then at last, a whimper. "He's dead..."

***

Blake hadn't noticed in his fit, but the narrow driveway to the trailer was packed with vehicles: Van's rusted heap of a sports car, his dad's truck, a brown van with curtains hung in the back windows, and a little gray hatchback with a Chrysler symbol on the grill.

Elden came quick once the call was made, and now stood beside his son holding his shoulders as he calmed down. Van and his dad stood next to them and another group of three watched from the little stoop of the trailer. Up the creek, they could see blue lights flashing off the trees and hillside.

Moments later, a State Police car arrived and rolled to a crunching halt at the end of the gravel. A short officer got out and walked towards them. He was a thin man with short blonde hair, looked to be in his mid-thirties.

"The local police are still up at the house," the officer said. "I'm Officer Bentley from the State Police Department." He shook Elden's hand and then Blake's. Van and his dad had taken a few steps back to join the stoop when the car arrived. "Who found him hanging?"

"My son found him," Elden said, rubbing Blake's shoulders firmly.

"If you don't mind me asking: son, what were you doing up there at that old house?" Officer Bentley said, kneeling to Blake. "And on Christmas to boot?"

Blake considered the truth and it jarred his stomach into violent spasms at remembering the knife in his hand. He thought of the crumpled letter with Cass's scrawl messing it, which was stuffed deep in his pocket.

"Cass was my friend," Blake said, and then dry-heaved. "I just wanted to wish him a Merry Christmas."

Officer Bentley cast a worried look at Elden.

"He was your friend?" he asked. "Son, that man's name wasn't Cass. His name was Randall Watson. Police have been looking for him for damn near eight months."

"What do you mean?" Blake asked.

"He was wanted for a laundry list of charges," Officer Bentley said to Elden. "But I won't get too far into the details in front of the boy. Let's just say he was bad news."

The words in Cass's letter wrote themselves in Blake's mind, and each once singed him. A great lump grew in his throat and he thought for a moment he would puke, but choked it back down and stood with his hands on his knees until he fell to the seat of his pants.

"Not trying to intrude, sir," Officer Bentley said. "But I'd be more careful who I let my boy run around with."

***

Greta held Blake tight as the day trudged on into the late afternoon, still gray and cloudy overhead. Her arms clung to his waste in the old swing on the front porch of Blake's house. Her head rested on his shoulder and neither spoke. Jenna sat at his other side with her arm around him, holding the wrinkled letter and hating that she had been right.

The front door clanged open and Elden stepped out and knelt down in front of them. He stroked Greta's hair and patted Blake's shoulder.

"Why don't you all come on in the house," he said. "We don't want to waste Christmas on *his* account, do we?"

He gave Jenna's thigh a squeeze and got back to his feet, returning indoors with a similar clang.

"He's right," Blake said, and the three of them entered the house still clinging to each other.

The house smelled prominently of pine and apple-scented candles. It was bursting with color shielding them all from the tragic gray outside. Greta had found the shoe strings on her porch with the tiny house trinket ready to attach and was wearing them in a new pair of shoes Blake had never seen before.

"Thank you for the gift," she said as they sat down in the floor in a corner near the pot-bellied stove. The chatter of Dianne, Patty, Elden, Arthur and Charlotte rang throughout the house as they attempted to salvage the holiday.

"It was nothing," Blake said. "I was happy to give it." He leaned to her and kissed her cheek, having discovered a new-found courage.

She took his hands in hers and said, "Let me grab your gift. I'll be right back." She got up and hurried off to the tree.

Blake watched her go and sighed, wishing he could smile.

"Here," she said, trotting back to him, sock feet patting the floor in gentle thumps. She handed him a small box and said, "Open it."

Blake took the gift as she dropped back down beside him. It was wrapped in shiny silver paper and tied with a blue ribbon that curled down the sides of the box. He pulled the ribbon and the complexity of the bow unfurled. He tore the paper to reveal an ordinary cardboard box.

"Go on," she said, smiling.

Blake pulled at the tape holding the cardboard together until it came off with a quick rasp. He opened the box and took out a smaller box that said Case Cutlery. The knife inside was wrapped in plastic and glowed like the shiny paper that had been concealing it. The box also contained oil and a new polish cloth folded into a tiny square, along with a sheet of paper folded next to it. Blake took it out and read.

It simply said. "I love you."

"My dad bought it. He knows what you'll use it for. He saw my old necklace," she said. "I'm not old enough to buy knives, I don't think. I gave him the money and picked it out though. Do you like it?"

"I love it," he said.

Blake smiled and was happy for just a moment. He had been shoving a stone uphill since finding Cass, and Greta's note was enough to push him over the top and allow him to wallow in good spirits for at least a little while.

"This thing is almost too pretty to cut wood with," he said.

Greta smiled at him. "I bet you'll break it in pretty quick."

Blake thought of the knife clenched in his hand as he stormed through the old house earlier that afternoon. He wondered about his intent and it scared him. A chill coursed through his body and his teeth smacked together a few times before he tightened his jaw to stop them.

"Blake, open mine," Jenna said. She tugged a stack of boxes to his side, all bound together with ribbon. Blake felt a twist of guilt, knowing he had nothing to give her.

He opened the boxes one at a time, wishing he had *anything* to give her in return. Each box contained a much-needed article of clothing: a brown and black striped sweater, two new pairs of jeans, a couple checked button-ups, and a pack of socks.

"I sure could use these," Blake said. "But... I didn't get you anything yet."

"You know I'm not worried about that," she said. "I just want to see you look spiffy for your girlfriend." She laughed.

Blake's ears got hot. Greta put her hand on his shoulder and kissed his cheek very quickly.

The night aged too fast and darkness overtook the gray sky at last. The get-together had died down some and folks sat around the living room sipping coffee or soft drinks. Blake, Greta and Jenna had gone upstairs and sat huddled in Blake's room with blankets and comforters draping their shoulders, telling stories and drinking hot cocoa. The clock on Blake's nightstand glowed a brilliant 8:29 in large, blocky red numbers.

Jenna was in the middle of telling Greta of their childhood, and Blake's untamed hair that always stood on end near the crown. But before she could finish her story, Patty came to the door and rapped gently on the enjambment.

"Blake, you have company downstairs," she said, forcing a thin-lipped smile.

"Company? Who is it?"

"Come down and see." And she was gone back into the darkness of the upstairs hallway.

Blake hurried down the steps and into the living room to find a short woman with graying hair sitting on the sofa wrapped in a long, black overcoat. Unfamiliar brown boots sat at the door on the rug with laces undone. She smiled at Blake when she saw him.

"Alfie Mae Piper," he said.

"Mmmhmm," she nodded.

"What are you doing here?"

"I stopped in at the library a couple of days ago to say hello to Bobbi Sanders and wish her Merry Christmas—she's a dear old friend. But all we talked about was how you had checked out one of my books and kept it for dang near a month." She smiled. "It does an old writer's heart good to see young people still interested in books."

"I couldn't put it down," he said. "I read *The Perfect Tree* like five times or something."

"I heard what happened." Her eyes drifted around the room, head shifting this way and that. "Up at that house. Mr. Bradley's old house."

Blake felt eyes on him and turned to see his parents eyeing them both, watching intently and listening.

"Yeah." He lower his gaze to the worn brown carpet, once thick and lush, now flat from heavy footfalls leading from point A to point B. "How did you know?"

"Blake, isn't it?" she inquired. "One thing you'll learn about Hemingford as you get older is word gets around. If a young'un smokes a cigarette, folks on the other side of the county'll know before the butt hits the ground." She patted the couch next to her and nodded for him to sit. Blake plopped onto the couch and rested his hands in his lap with fingers locked together. His parents turned and left the room, rejoining the get-together which had moved to the kitchen. "I knew he was living there," Alfie said.

"What?" Blake perked up and stared at her wide-eyed.

"I go up there from time to time, just to visit the old place. After all, it was the last place Mr. Bradley ever saw before... doing what he did. And one time I stood looking at the house, but noticed somebody was looking back—a fuzz-faced man was looking at me from one of the windows."

"Did he talk to you?"

"He did. At first it upset me that somebody was hiding out in Mr. Bradley's house. But the poor thing was about starved to death, living off of what he could scrounge around and steal from abandoned houses and farms. For some reason, I wasn't afraid of him."

"You should've been," Blake said. "Everybody should've been." He gazed around, ensuring no prying ears were about. "He was a monster."

Alfie gasped. "Did you know him?"

"Yeah, I thought he was my friend."

Alfie thumbed the strap of her large purse at her side.

"You know, I was just a few steps away from finding exactly what you found."

"What do you mean?"

"When Mr. Bradley disappeared, I went up there looking for him. I was just a little girl at the time. I figured he was sick and bed-ridden, or something like that. I searched the house and didn't find anything but a mess. Mr. Bradley was nowhere to be seen. I'm so thankful I didn't go out into the backyard. Neighbors found him there a few days after, hangin' from an old, oak tree."

Cass filled Blake's mind. He could see his limbs hanging lifeless from his body, and that horrid look on his face, mouth gaping open, the whites of his eyes glassed over.

"At least you can remember Mr. Bradley and think good thoughts," Blake said. "Cass did some bad stuff."

"He did good stuff too, didn't he? That old fellow seemed like he'd give just about anybody the shirt off his back if they really needed it."

Blake hung his head and sank into the couch. He thought about telling Alfie about the letter, but the thought made his insides quake.

"The bad stuff is just harder to take back. Much more finite than the good," Alfie said. "Good stuff is easier to forget, I reckon."

For a moment, anger ballooned up in Blake's head and threatened to burst. But he looked at her and calmly said, "I guess you're right."

"Think of it like this. When you look at a tree, you can see what it's good for. Some of it's good, some of it's bad, and people are the same way." She sighed. "It's hard, but if the man ever done right by you, try to remember him for that, if you remember him at all."

"Okay," Blake said. "But I don't know if I can."

Alfie didn't ask anything. She reached into her purse and took out a large, rectangular gift, wrapped in simple white paper. "I suspect you know what this is." She got to her feet and went to the door and stooped to tie her boots. "Tell your family I said 'Merry Christmas.'"

She left, easing the door closed behind her.

Blake stood in silence clutching the gift that he knew was *Afternoonls.*

***

After everyone left, and the house lay still, Blake placed the book, still wrapped in the coarse paper, on his nightstand and set his tiny alarm clock for 5:30. He turned in and covered up with his thick blankets, and thought he could still taste Greta's kiss on his lips. He was glad his parents had gotten along well with Vernon and Charlotte. He needed them to get along. It would definitely make things easier for him and Greta.

The last thing he thought before sleep surprisingly had nothing to do with Cass or the darkness that surrounded everything he had touched, but of Jenna and what gift he would make her the next day. He would work on it constantly until it was perfect. She deserved his best work.

He rose early with the persistent chiming of his alarm. The house was cold and he could see wisps of his breath leave his mouth before he even threw the covers back. He got up and dressed warmly: wool socks, long johns, jeans, a sweater and a thick jacket. He tiptoed downstairs carrying his boots, and put them on just before stepping out the door into the cold, so as not to wake the house with his clomping about.

The old oak tree in his own backyard gave him chills, and as he cut a chunk from one of its limbs he thought, *I may never look at trees the same way again.*

He set to whittling on the back porch despite the cold. He carved away the skin of the tree in long, thin strips and chipped at the flesh until, with time, the wood began to take the shape of a small heart. Once the heart was finished, he would sand it smooth and etch a distinct "J" into the center. He just hoped Jenna had a chain to put it on seeing as how he had trouble locating one for Greta's new necklace.

It was about 7:30 when the heart was nearing finish. Thankfully, due to the short time he had to make it, the heart didn't require as much detail as the owl or the tree or most other things he carved, but he thought Jenna would love it. He eased up to his room, leaving everyone else to sleep in if they wanted too. His family hardly ever took a day to sleep past sunrise and he felt they deserved it, especially Jenna. He looked in on her as he passed the door to the guest room and her peaceful, sleeping face warmed him and brought a smile to his lips. The smile forced his lips to crack, chapped from sitting out in the morning freeze.

He searched his room for sandpaper to no avail. He eased back downstairs and slipped the keys to the truck, house and tool shed from the tiny hook by the kitchen door. *Surely, Dad will have some in the shed.*

He ran to the tool shed. Jenna would be awake soon. As would his dad, who would kill him if he caught him in the shed where he kept all of his expensive tools. He forced the key into the time-worn lock and, being stiff in the cold, it turned with a little coaxing. Inside, the shed stank of oil and sweat and gasoline. He rummaged the drawers of a great tool chest against the far wall, finding wrenches, ratchets, a hammer and nails, and a few spare spark plugs, all strewn about with no order. He tried the

Kenneth S. Harris

small drawers at the bottom hoping to find just a scrap of sandpaper if not a whole roll.

Blake opened a tiny drawer, not three inches wide, and fell back onto the freezing floor at the sight of what it contained, taking the drawer along with him. It tumbled to the ground with a jarring clank. Blake stopped breathing and his body shook and went numb at the tips. Inside the drawer rested a tiny wooden owl on an old silver chain.